THIS IS LIFE

BRENDA BROSTER

Bloomington, IN Milton Keynes, UK

AuthorHouse™
1663 Liberty Drive, Suite 200
Bloomington, IN 47403
www.authorhouse.com
Phone: 1-800-839-8640

AuthorHouse™ UK Ltd.
500 Avebury Boulevard
Central Milton Keynes, MK9 2BE
www.authorhouse.co.uk
Phone: 08001974150

This is a work of fiction. Although some incidents are loosely based on real events and the author's experience, any similarity or resemblance to actual persons, living or dead, is conicidental. The characters within this book are the creations of the author's imagination.

First published by AuthorHouse 11/16/2006

ISBN: 978-1-4259-7753-5 (sc)

Printed in the United States of America
Bloomington, Indiana

This book is printed on acid-free paper.

This book is dedicated to all those people
who find modern life such a struggle.

TABLE OF CONTENTS

DESTINY

Mary looked at her watch yet again. It was eleven o'clock. Still he was not home. The children were still up, squabbling as usual. She shouted at them "Go to bed, NOW". "You should be asleep". It did not occur to her that the children should have been in bed long ago. She had needed their company; so much better than the loneliness of being alone evening after evening.

If only he would come home in the evenings, everything would be better. He could help with the children. They could cook a meal together, have a glass of wine, talk. But he never did, and everything was always left to her. Her teaching job was demanding. She spent the day in school, then had to run round after their own children, cook, clean, wash, iron. Surely he could help. Her teaching hours were sometimes inordinately long. There was always worry about money, rows when he did come home. In order to cut back, meals were usually pasta with a sauce of some kind. And now the telephone had been switched off (another unpaid bill) and the gas heating was on the blink, so they were all cold. And the school fees bill had come in this morning, along with a notification from the building society that the mortgage had not been paid – yet again.

Mary wrapped herself in a duvet and curled up in the armchair. It was all his fault. Why did he not get a proper job; why did he not earn enough money to support them all properly. She kept telling him he had to earn more; it was his duty to support his family. She started crying and, once the tears started to flow, they became a torrent. Why, she sobbed, is he such a useless husband? Why does he not come home? For a woman, there's something very satisfying about tears. They assuage the soul. And if we are driven to tears, then we must be victims. "It's all his fault. He never provides for us. He's probably off again, out with his friends, spending all our money". Mary determined to wait up for him. So she sat there, sniffing, crying, occasionally dozing, wrapped in the duvet, feeling sorry for herself.

He was out, pacing the streets, shivering when he stopped walking. It was cold. A first impression would have been of a man smartly dressed but, on closer inspection, his coat was threadbare, his collar and cuffs were worn, and his shoes had holes in the soles. He had ten pounds left in his pocket to see him through the week. He would walk home; it was only six miles, the exercise would do him good, and it would warm him up.

He had arrived at the office at seven-thirty that morning, and hung around until eight-thirty in the evening – not that he had much to do, but he was resisting the prospect of getting home. Now it was late; with luck he would not get home until the early hours, and Mary would be asleep. He would not have to face her. He started walking again. His thoughts, as ever, were pessimistic. The children always needed money, the car needed petrol in it, and Angela needed a new coat. Mary insisted they buy it from Harrods – only the best would ever do for the children. Ever since they were born, all their clothes had come from Harrods. "What about Marks & Spencers" he thought. "Why can't we be like other families and shop in sensible places.

When he eventually arrived home, he was hungry and weary. All he could think about was getting something to eat and then sleep. As he put his key in the lock, very gently so as not to waken anyone, Mary sat bolt upright in her chair. She had heard him. She waited until he was inside the door and it had shut. "James" she called "In here". He stopped in his tracks like a frightened rabbit. Sighing, he made his was reluctantly to the sitting room door. Her eyes were swollen with crying. "Where have you been" she demanded. He said nothing. He knew what was to come. It was a regular pattern. "You never let us know what you are doing. You are never here. You never make enough money. All these bills to pay" (scooping them up off the coffee table and throwing them at him). Picking them up, he asked "what's to eat? I'm starving". "Nothing". She said. "If you want food, you have to pay for it". Putting the bills down without looking at them, he turned his back on her and made his way to the kitchen. She sank back into the duvet. She started to cry again. The tone of her crying irritated him intensely. It was a sort of high-pitched wailing noise, monotonous, and continuous.

He found some cereal and milk and, pouring it into a bowl, ate ravenously.

Then he went to the broom cupboard, pulled out a single mattress (one of the blow-up kind), blew it up, and put it down in the hallway. He had been sleeping in the hallway for months. He simply could not face going to bed with Mary where he would yet again be faced with a constant stream of complaint, blame, nagging. As for sex! Well, that had gone out of the window long ago. He could no longer fancy her to save his life. He had tried sleeping in one of the boys' beds whilst they were at school, but Mary would not let him. She said he smelt and it upset the boys to come home to a smelly bed. He got out the sleeping bag.

Fully clothed and wrapped in her duvet, Mary sat in the chair all night. It was a sort of challenge to him "Here I am, sitting up all night, unable to sleep, and all because of you".

Nothing had worked out as she had planned it. She had wanted James to become a teacher, like her, work with children, bring home a regular income, and spend time with their own children in the holidays. She had it all mapped out. Eventually he would become a headmaster. But it had all gone horribly wrong. And she was SO miserable!

It was all his fault, of course!

Next morning, he was up at six-thirty a.m., ready to leave at seven for the office. There was just time to shower (cold water!), shave, iron his shirt, and he was off. Despite having to get to school herself, she wanted a conversation. He avoided it. As he left, he shouted through the half open front door "I'll try to get home earlier tonight. We can talk then". Maybe she would have time to calm down. He simply could not cope with those constant tears.

Mary went to the bathroom, splashed cold water over her eyes, automatically following her daily routine. She felt terrible. Her brain was like cotton wool. It was all his fault! Why was he so cruel? He never took any notice of her. He was so selfish. She dressed and went down to the kitchen.

Angela was already down. She had always been an early riser. Of the two girls, she was her mother's favourite. In reality, temperamentally, of all the children, she was most like her mother. Like Mary, she resorted easily to tears. And like Mary, her view of life was very black and white. Things were either right or they were wrong. Phrases like "mitigating circumstances" or "under duress" were alien to them.

Angela now saw that her mother had been crying again. "So he's been home, then?" she asked. Mary simply nodded, and the tears crept back into her eyes. At that point Mark came down. He saws the tears and hugged his mother wordlessly. Of the twins, he was the more sensitive. Anthony, the older twin, was the extrovert. And because he was more extrovert, ergo, he was not sensitive. That is how Mary thought. And Rosemary, of course, was just like her father – always getting into and causing trouble. And SHE certainly was not sensitive at all.

The children would have to stay at home alone today. It was normal during the holidays when Mary was tutoring. Angela would be in charge. She, at fourteen, was the eldest. The twins were twelve, and Rosemary was ten. They had strict instructions not to open the door to anyone. They all had homework to do (even in the holidays there was no let-up), and their music practice. The girls played the piano, Mark the violin, and Anthony the viola. Both boys were, Mary thought, considerably gifted, and she was spending a fortune sending them to the top teachers money could buy. Mark actually needed a better violin, but it would cost many thousands of pounds, and she knew she would have a battle with James over that.

That evening, Mary had just got in when James arrived home. She was astonished to see him. He had not been home so early for months. She started cooking supper – pasta again, with tomatoes and onion. James said "We cannot go on like this. We have got to talk". Mary started crying. She said it was the onions. "We'll talk after supper" he said. Then he concentrated on the children, teasing them in his light-hearted way whilst they laid the table, joking with them. They were laughing. They did not seem to notice how unhappy she was. James and the children continued their banter during supper. Mary ate in silence.

After they had eaten, they left the children to clear up, following which, they were told, they could watch television. She and James went into the sitting room. They sat down. There was silence. James always found it difficult to talk to Mary. She would either explode into recrimination or burst into tears, and he never knew which to expect. He dreaded both. Eventually, he managed to say "Our biggest problem is money and, even between us, we cannot earn enough to pay the mortgage as well as school fees for four children. That's the crux of the matter". Mary sat, ashen-faced. He continued "It's either school fees or mortgage, but we can't do both. What we should do is sell the house – get something smaller". Still she said nothing. "Well?" he asked. "It's up to you" she said. "You're the one who insisted on buying this house. I'd have been happier with something smaller. It was your decision to buy it, so it's up to you to find the money. You just have to earn more. We're not moving".

He was getting nowhere. "Mary, we've had this conversation so many times before. When will you accept that it's not that easy to earn more money out there? I'm already holding down two jobs – day and evening. I can't do any more". She looked up. She noticed he was wearing a new tie. "Where did you get that tie? How can you talk about money like this, and buy all those new clothes? Mark needs a new violin. Angela needs a new coat. You're just so selfish." And she started to cry. "Fuck you" James shouted. He stormed out of the room. The children, of course, were biddable. She could manipulate them, control them; but James was a law unto himself. She never knew what he would do next. It really bothered her. He went and sat with the children watching television. Accustomed to all the rows and the moods, they did not say anything. It was typical of Mary, he brooded, to pick up on a tie when he was trying to discuss the essentials. He had bought the tie in a charity shop that morning because a chap in the office had spilled coffee down the one he was originally wearing. That night, he slept in the hallway again.

The following morning, James could not wait to get back to the office. The secretaries there were sweet, very pretty – some of them, anyway, and he could flirt with them, laugh and remember that he was a man, after all. His colleagues were decent people, too. All in the same boat, scrambling to earn a crust; it was humour which kept them going.

That night, rather than go home and face all the recrimination, James chose to stay with one of the other consultants, Oliver, who let him sleep on the sofa whenever he liked. It was a relief. Oliver let him stay for a whole week. James kept his mobile 'phone switched off, so that Mary could not contact him. He had done this on many occasions previously.

He was in an impossible situation. He was not earning enough money. The company he was seconded to, Allied Botcher, invoiced him every month for office space and so on, and he knew full well that they made a handsome profit out of his overhead charges, just as they did on every consultant they deigned to allow to sell their products. And there were clawbacks too. His colleague, Andrew Dober, had just had a £200,000 clawback. That meant that the company to whom Andrew had sold a pension scheme only six months ago had gone to the wall, and Andrew had to pay back £200,000 to Allied Botcher (commission earned on five years' pension contributions for all employees of that company). James smiled wryly. Andrew had been over the moon when he brought that piece of business in, but he would be in trouble now. Because James knew he had already spent it – all of it, mostly in paying off debts incurred during the lean days. Like it or not, that was the nature of the beast. There were those who would say "If you don't like the heat in the kitchen, get out". But where to? And what else could he do?

James was fully aware that, as an ex army officer of lower rank when he left the army, there were not many resources open to him. Perhaps he should not have left the army, but that, in itself, was a source of contention at home. Mary had hated him being in the army, and had done everything possible to persuade him to leave. She had been very obstructive, actually, refusing to attend events, refusing to move with him. Eventually, partly because of her, and partly because he needed to make more money, he left.

He never quite knew whether it was predominantly Mary or his own sense of inadequacy which persuaded him to leave. Inadequacy. Now there's a word. Yes, he did often feel inadequate, probably because Mary was always telling him he was useless, worthless, an embarrassment, a waste of space. He would never be able to match up to her aspirations as a husband.

James found an advertisement in a newspaper "Telephone sales people needed. £7.00 per hour, evenings". He telephoned and got the job. He could work in the evenings and make £7.00 per hour. It also meant he would not have to spend the evenings at home.

Mary, herself a talented pianist, had started giving piano lessons to children in the area, as well as tutoring. A good teacher, she was much in demand, and now worked five evenings a week. She rarely got home before 10.00 p.m. so, with James away in the evenings too, the children had to fend for themselves. There was the inevitable fighting and back-biting found in any family where children are left to their own devices for fourteen hours a day. And still there was never enough money. It was a relief during term time that the boys were at boarding school. But that meant that, every weekend, Mary tore off up the motorway to spend Sundays with the boys. Usually she dragged the girls along as well, much against their wishes.

Occasionally James went too.

One weekend Mary said "James, we've got to have a holiday. The children need a holiday". "We can't afford it" he said. "We're going, whether you like it or not" she said. "Then you'll have to go without me. I'm too busy at the office".

"There's a Regimental Ball" he said "We've got an invitation". "We're not going" she said "I've nothing to wear". "What about that Ball gown you wore to the Christmas Ball last year?" he asked. "That Christmas Ball was three years ago, and I couldn't possibly wear that dress again. I'd have to have a new one. I'm simply not going. Besides, you're such an embarrassment in public". "What do you mean – an embarrassment?" he asked. "You just are. You're so embarrassing".

Mary, lacking self confidence herself, found it difficult to attend any public event. She agonised for hours over what to wear, what to do, what to say. She needed a new gown to boost her self confidence. It was anathema to her to attend a Ball without a new gown.

That was part of their problem. She was never able to express herself properly to James, just as he was never able to express himself at all to her. They lived under the same roof but, once the initial passions of youth had died down, they had nothing in common. Aware of the great void, but unable to understand or explain it, they took it out on each other.

Mary's view of life is that men and women marry, and have children – procreation is the purpose of marriage. The wife looks after the children, and the husband is the breadwinner. Once a husband and wife have bonded and produced children, nothing on earth can come between them. Simple! Her own parents' marriage had been a loveless disaster, so perhaps her ideas are idealistic on the basis of what she wants rather than reality.

James has a different viewpoint. He never wanted children really, at least not in the early days. But Mary wanted children, and it was the thing which people did, so he went along with it. James, very much a youngest and adored son, had been indulged by his parents, but not allowed to socialise in case he got into bad company. His elder brother had done very well in the army, and had been held up as a pillar of the community to the young and impressionable James. He should emulate his wonderful brother in everything, and he would go far. He did not leave home until he joined the army, going from one controlled environment into another. Young and very immature, he was not ready, when he married, for responsibility.

James and Mary had played together as children. Their mothers had met and become friends whilst on holiday. Both families regularly holidayed in Norfolk. James and Mary spent many happy hours sailing together in Mirrors, Toppers, and various other small boats. It was not long before the childhood relationship became something else. Both mothers were delighted and positively encouraged the relationship, albeit that the children were still only sixteen.

For the next couple of years James and Mary looked forward to their long languid holidays in Norfolk. By modern standards, it was a little strange that they continued to holiday with their parents, but it was economically convenient, and they both had an ulterior motive – they could see each other again. Each summer the relationship became more highly charged, more passionate.

Then Mary went off to teacher training college. James, however, still lived with his parents, finding a local job which was definitely not career oriented. He did not know what he wanted to do.

It was difficult to resist the combined pressure of Mary, her parents, and his own parents. They all seemed to think there was nothing else in life but marriage. An only son of older parents, James was accustomed to having his life run for him by them. Eventually he gave in. He even began to like the idea of marriage. Nonetheless, he would not agree to a specific date. He could not afford an engagement ring. He was twenty-two.

In the meantime, contrary to Mary's wishes, James joined the army. He was commissioned into an auspicious regiment. James absolutely loved the "action man" lifestyle of the army. He was posted overseas for six months at a time, and saw little of Mary. He invited Mary over to Germany for various regimental occasions, a passing out parade, a Regimental Ball. She never came. He learned early that everything they did had to be on her terms. She continued to press for a wedding date. He resisted.

One day he said he did not, after all, want to get married. He did not say "not at all". He said "not just yet". When she saw that James was determined and that tears did not work, she threatened to jump off a bridge and kill herself if he did not marry her. Her parents now got involved. They insisted. James gave in, and agreed a date. He had a vague suspicion that suicide might run in the family. James still tried to back out of the wedding. He was not ready to settle down.

They were married with full military honours.

Mary was deliriously happy. James enjoyed the sex but, otherwise, was disinterested.

The children came along fast and furious. The first, Angela, was born just twelve months after they were married. James was away from home most of the time: in Northern Ireland, Germany, Norway. Mary would not go with him. She stayed at home with Angela. Actually, she would not get involved in any part of his army life. As an officer, his wife was expected to play her part. Mary refused. Consequently, they became more and more estranged, and James started to play away – not often, just occasionally. He volunteered for exercises overseas whenever he could – unaware that he was subconsciously escaping domestic life. Without doubt, he loved Angela, but babies puked, cried constantly, were always damp, demanding. The less he had to do with them the better. Occasional clean, dry cuddles were wonderful, but that was the full extent of his involvement.

James, in the army, was of necessity away from home a great deal, and still only twenty-four years old. It was not an auspicious start to a marriage.

Mary, a timid and self-effacing but stubborn girl, had to learn to fend for herself. She did not have a good example of motherhood to follow. Her own mother had been a "musician", playing in an illustrious orchestra, as had her father. So Mary had been brought up by an ever changing army of au pairs. Her parents had always been engrossed in their own lives, their music, to the detriment of their children. Whereas they adored Mary's older brother, they gave her scant attention.

The result was that she spent the rest of her life trying to please her mother, earn the approval of her mother. She never felt that she got it. Her mother had never set her parameters of behaviour. There was always discussion "If you do this, that will be the consequence; if you do that, on the other hand, the consequence will be different", but never did she offer an opinion. So Mary never knew what her mother really thought. Her father was indifferent in that wholly self-absorbed way of a lot of musicians. Her elder brother was adored and did very much his own thing. Mary learned to get her own way, to be noticed, by crying, by threatening, by manipulating.

In her loneliness, she had mentally formed a picture of the ideal husband. He was always biddable, always shared all tasks equally, was always there for her. He was kind and considerate. He was sensitive and had a strong feminine side, although he was very masculine and strong. He would be the breadwinner, providing for all their needs, whilst she raised their little family, looked after the home, did the cooking and the gardening in their idyllic little cottage. Every girl's dream! But only a dream.

Mary's exposure to life prior to marriage had been minimal. She was quite determined that she would always shop at Harrods, as her mother had, and that her children would all be educated privately. After all, she had never known anything different. It did not occurr to her to think about "the cost". One did not discuss nasty things like money. One just accepted that these were the things one did, and her husband would provide.

Meantime James was having a pretty good time in Norway, where he skied daily with his troops, sailed, parachuted. James loved the outdoor life. He loved competition, proving himself. He had a way with him. He built rapport with his men, and they respected him.

Not particularly large, he was tough and fair. He was good at logistics and an excellent tactician. He was also very good-looking.

Inevitably there were the few Norwegian girls he established relationships with, one in particular. It was fun, it was light-hearted. It took him away from all the care and responsibility of family life, of children, and of financial worries. He could drink, dance, make love, without pressure. He found in these relationships an escape which kept him sane.

He came home on leave. He and Mary found it slightly difficult to adjust to being together again after six months' absence, but they managed to rub along rather well. They were still young and the mutual attraction which had brought them together in the first place was still there. He was posted in the UK now for a couple of years, and so they decided to buy a house of their own.

They found a little house which needed a great deal done to it. It was all they could afford. Actually, it was a dump. But James felt he could do something with it. Ever the practical man with his hands, it did not constitute a major problem in his eyes. It was exciting. They pulled together and life was harmonious for quite a time. They worked hard and created a warm and friendly, albeit somewhat cramped, little cottage.

Mary announced that she was pregnant again, expecting twins. This time James felt more able to cope, although Mary was scared at the prospect of having to look after the children on her own if he were posted away again. He assured Mary that he would be in the UK for at least another eighteen months. Mary concentrated on the garden whilst Angela toddled around, and James went off to work daily, returning in the evenings. There was another Regimental do, and yet again Mary would not go. She felt that everyone would be looking at her. She was so big now, with the twins. So James went alone. It was inconceivable that an officer would not attend any regimental function.

The twins were born without mishap. James was thrilled that he had two sons. Every man wants a son. But two! He felt slightly greedy.

Then came the interrupted nights, two babies demanding attention, and Angela, feeling left out, also demanding. Every time he came home to the little house, there were demanding children, toys littering the floor. There was nowhere to put them away. Mary was constantly tired, always rushing around, trying to cope. James was useless with nappies and things. He was good at cuddling the babies, quietening them down, but that was all. She resented that he was not a "modern" father. He did not come home from work, take over the feeding, bathing and so on, She felt he should be more helpful. He felt that, suffering from lack of sleep because of the babies, he had done a hard day's work, and wanted peace and quiet.

They called the babies Anthony and Mark, and then thought about Mark Anthony and all he represented. But that had not occurred to them when they were thinking of names. It was really Mary who chose the names. James just agreed – anything for a peaceful life. But he did not mind the names. They were as good as any.

Her day was so full: get the babies up (and Angela, at two, was still a baby), go shopping (which entailed getting all the babies dressed in warm clothing getting them into the car, with the buggy, getting them out of the car at the other end, shopping with three small children in tow, and all the loading and unloading of the car again on the way home). There were meals to prepare, the washing, the ironing, the housework, the gardening and, to make a little extra money, she was also baking cakes to sell. She never had a moment to sit down, to reflect. She had to watch Angela who, having had undivided attention so far, was prone to poke or bash the twins. She was exhausted. When the twins were six months old, she realised she was pregnant again. When Rosemary was born, Mary and James, in their tiny cottage, had four children under the age of four.

That is when the bickering really started. Mary and James, both worn out with the children, were taking it out on each other. He started staying longer at work. She questioned him. Why did he need to be at the barracks all the time? He was needed at home. His children never saw him. She needed help. Large gaps in communication were growing between them. He no longer bothered to tell her when there were regimental occasions to which she could accompany him. He went alone. On such occasions, he would ask a pretty young female officer to accompany him. Mary, on the other hand, became more and more engrossed with the children. She hardly noticed, now, whether James was there or not.

Children are expensive. Finance became more and more of a problem. The baked cakes were bringing in some pocket money, but that was all it was. The pressure was intense. Mary and James both dreaded the constant quarrelling when he got home. Mary decided that they must see a marriage guidance counsellor. She could not, for the life of her, see why James was not content with his little family. He could not, for the life of him, see why Mary wanted nothing more. The marriage guidance counsellor was a waste of time. Mary took it all very seriously. James paid lip service.

On Angela's fourth birthday, Mary insisted on sending her to an expensive private school. James gave in, as usual – anything for a peaceful life. Uniform had to be bought – at Harrods, of course. He was a Lieutenant, on a Lieutenant's salary! The following year, the twins started at the same school, and the year after that, Rosemary. James had been promoted. There was a little more money. But still! Four children at private school on a Captain's salary, and a mortgage to pay! James and Mary were twenty-seven years old. Mary went to work – as a teacher to help support the children. She also took in outwork which she could do at home. She was permanently exhausted.

And so the real treadmill of their life started. There was never, ever enough money. Mary adhered to the old adage that it is the role of the father to be breadwinner, and, in her view, it was up to the father to provide the lifestyle to which they aspired. Her argument was that, as James had agreed to send the children to a private school, it was up to him to provide the fees. As he had agreed to take out a mortgage and buy a house, it was up to him to find the premiums each month. She did all she could to help, but never saw these as joint liabilities.

James, needing to get away from it all, volunteered for duty in Northern Ireland. To this day, he will not discuss what happened there. He is very good at accents. He has Irish looks, and could easily pass for an Irishman. James is a crack shot. He went under cover, working for the army. He was away for eighteen months. When he returned he was a changed man.

And Mary was a changed woman.

James left the Army, and went into insurance. Self-employed, he reasoned, he could earn a lot more money. But the insurance world is very difficult. One literally has to carry all one's own expenses, pay for desk space, telephone bills, travel, stationary. It is a commission-based industry. He only made money when prospective clients actually invested through him. James was pretty good at the job – he was intelligent, educated, and charming. Clients generally liked and trusted him. He earned considerably more than when in the army, but still it was never enough. Mary constantly reminded him of that. To be fair to her, she worked all the hours she could trying to raise more money to pay for the childrens' education. Somewhere along the line, she had lost the concept that there is more to life than a private education for one's children. When the children got older, she was rarely at home – always out giving "private" tutorials to slower pupils. James , too, was rarely at home – he had taken an evening job – "telephone sales" – to help pay the school fees.

Nevertheless, the monthly pay packets still ran out long before the end of the month. Mary cut down on food, on electricity, on gas. If cold, the children were told to put on more clothes. If hungry, there was bread, there was pasta, there was cereal. Night after night, bread and pasta and cereal.

The children were left alone evening after evening. The twins were at boarding school, but the girls were at home. They lived in the city now, and were forbidden to open the door to anyone. They did not bring friends home. Mary and James, in all their married life, had only twice had people in to dinner, and then they were fellow teachers of Mary's, and she had sweated over a hot stove for hours and hours preparing everything to perfection. The experience had been a chore, not a pleasure. Reality is that they had no social life, no friends, and no time for either. And they started to avoid each other.

The children had become accustomed to their father never turning up for prize days, parents' evenings, sports days. Their mother could always be relied upon to be there for them when they needed her, but he always said he was too busy working. He stopped going with them on family holidays – too busy working again. Mary thought he just did not want to be with his family. Reality is that he was so desperate to make some money somehow that he forgot there is another life. The children had learned to live without their father.

Mary and James were effectively living separate lives. They had forgotten how to communicate – not that they had ever really been able to. James had long since started to avoid her. It was easier that way. Conflict, confrontation had always been anathema to him.

Neither of them will ever know how the crunch came or when it came. Mary had retreated more and more into her own world, and James had retreated more and more into his. The children were somehow stuck in the middle, and Mary did her best to be that ideal mother she had always dreamed of having herself. What she did not realise was that, by trying so hard, she was actually suffocating the children and making them so dependent on her that they would not be able to break the apron strings. Then, again, there are those who would say that she knew exactly what she was doing, that she was terrified of losing their love and affection, and was deliberately, albeit subconsciously, steering them away from any affection they had for their father.

She now criticised him openly and regularly, in front of the children. Her attitude was that the children should be privy to everything in family life, the good and the bad. In front of them she would tell James over and over again that he was useless, a waste of space, an embarrassment. She still would not accompany him to any events or functions. She said he was too much of an embarrassment. He, on the other hand, told her she had let herself go, was fat, was dowdy. She dressed like her mother. They each undermined the other until neither had any self-confidence left. He would lose his temper, swear and shout, slam doors. If the children were in the way, he would even lash out at them on occasion. She always assumed the patient martyr role, and sank into deep silences which lasted for days. James could not stand that.

He stayed away from home more and more often. He had plenty of friends who would put him up. Sometimes they were ladies, but mostly they were fellow workers from the office. And he stayed away for longer and longer periods. When he did come home, Mary was usually busy teaching or taking the children somewhere. When they were both home together the atmosphere was stilted, stiff, neither knowing what to say to the other.

The children got on with their lives. He became more and more superfluous to their needs, and he noticed it. Encouraged subconsciously by Mary, they made him feel more and more like a lodger. He had not felt for a long time that he was a part of the family.

After yet another row, he stormed out of the house. Mary, accustomed by now to his absences, did not consider it unusual that, after ten days, he had still not returned. His mobile was, of course, switched off. She did not know where he was, she could not contact him. He telephoned her saying that he needed time and space. He said they needed to talk, and took her out to dinner, but they did not talk about anything serious, just small talk. Mary wondered what she was doing there. James simply could not bring himself to admit that he wanted to leave her.

Nothing was achieved. Time went by. He never did come back. James found that each time he thought about returning to the family home, he simply could not do it. Weeks, months, went by, and it became harder and harder even to contemplate a return. He took Mary out to dinner several times to try and explain, but found that he could not tell her what he thought, what he felt. The dinner was wasted.

James stayed with friends, relatives, anyone rather than go home. Eventually, he took up with another woman. He did not tell Mary, 'though. He was riddled with guilt about his behaviour towards his family, but could not bring himself to do anything to rectify the situation. The guilt preyed on his mind. Eventually, in the throes of a breakdown, he lost both his jobs. Now he could not even send money home. He tried to contact the children. They would not have anything to do with him. Unable to contact his family, and unable to get work, he was in utter despair. He had a breakdown.

Mary, eventually understanding that James would not return, decided to carry on life as normally as possible, just as she had done when James was away so often with the army. From the day that he left the house, his name was never again mentioned in it. She and the children did not talk about him. They simply obliterated him from their lives. The family telephone line was changed and made ex-directory, the children's mobile 'phone numbers were all changed. They were effectively incommunicado.

In the acrimonious divorce Mary got the house, the children, the chattels. James lost everything, except the family debts. Mary had stalled and adjourned divorce proceedings for years. James did not understand why. When it finally happened, Rosemary, the youngest child, was over the age of sixteen. James had no rights as a parent. If Rosemary or any of the others did not want to see him, he could do nothing about it. Now he understood why Mary had refused to divorce until Rosemary was over sixteen.

James had no way of communicating with his family other than by letter. Like so many men, he was not a prestigious letter-writer. He sent cards, letters, presents for birthdays and Christmas – never got an acknowledgement or even a "thank-you". He always made sure he sent the children his address, his own telephone number, begged them to get in touch, assured them of his love, how much he missed them. Following these missives he would rush to the door every time the post was delivered, rush trembling to the telephone when it rang. But there never was a response. He even went up to the house and dropped notes through the letter box – just to ensure they were received. Nothing!

His girlfriend wrote to the children, begging them to contact their father. She, too, sent them cards, presents.

Presents were kept, but cards and letters were returned. She received a letter from Mary's solicitor threatening legal action should she ever try to contact the children again.

Six years later, James was offered the opportunity of starting up a business in the Far East. This was the best offer of work he was ever likely to get. He had scraped a living over the past few years by taking any menial jobs he could get, but none was satisfactory. His girlfriend told him to "go for it". He had nothing left to lose.

He made a last huge effort to contact his family before he went. The children were now in their twenties. One day his mobile 'phone rang. It was Rosemary. She called him "James", not Daddy. She harangued him, swore at him, told him he was not their father any longer. But she did agree to see him. When he put the 'phone down after the conversation, he sobbed.

He met Rosemary and did not recognise her. She was with a friend. The meeting did not go well. She was so hostile it took his breath away. She told him that, as far as the boys and Angela were concerned, he was dead. His only consolation was that he now had Rosemary's mobile number. He felt it was a start.

James knew he had been a somewhat indifferent father (like so many), he had been a womaniser (but discreetly). He had not been violent, abusive, an alcoholic. He admitted he had frequently forgotten such events as end of term plays, concerts, that sort of thing. Mary had always been very conscientious about such things. By and large he considered himself to be a pretty normal father. He could not understand what he had done to make his children loathe him so thoroughly.

Three days later he flew off to the Far East, not knowing whether he would ever see his children again. And Mary and the children continue to live their lives as if he never existed.

JOSIE

Josie was on the beach at Brean. It was the beginning of spring; the horrible cold frosty nights had ended, and she was warm enough. She pulled her old leather coat closely around her and sat down. Sea mist was rising out of the incoming tide, and through the mist she could see Wales across the bay. There had always been something mystical about Wales – the beauty, the legends, the song. Seeing it's coastline like this only added to the magic. The sun's watery rays were trying to break through the mist casting silver light on the gentle incoming breakers. Here at least the world appeared to be calm and at peace. There was a slight breeze off the sea. Josie caught her straying hair and tucked it back under her woolly hat. It was still not really warm enough to sit. She started walking. The beach was so long, she could not see where it ended. Her boots were sturdy and she had had a good meal that day. Life was not that bad. She enjoyed strolling along the beach not knowing where she was going. It would have been better if Gay were still with her. Gay had been the most loyal and affectionate companion, but she had eventually died, and Josie had buried her amongst the roses. Gay had been her very best friend, and she did not want another dog after that.

As she progressed along the beach, Josie became aware of the caravans in caravan parks running parallel to it, miles and miles, avenues and avenues of caravan parks, all standing silent in serried ranks. This place must be awful in summer but, with luck, it would serve a purpose tonight. She met a dog walker; they smiled at each other. A young girl trotted by on a pretty little Arab. "Bit plump, though" thought Josie. This was life as she liked it. It would soon be dusk.

And then dusk slid stealthily over the land. Josie slid stealthily through the avenues of caravans. Silently she turned door handles, always keeping a sharp eye out for open windows – any way she could get in! Her lifestyle of late ensured that her senses were acutely sharpened. A dog barked nearby. Josie froze. It quietened down, and she continued her quest. Then she spotted it – a window left slightly ajar, probably to let the air circulate. Deftly, she pulled it as wide as she could, but it was too high up. She found a portable step from another caravan, climbed up and, with surprising agility, wriggled through, pulling her small rucksack in behind her. Putting her rucksack down, she pulled the window to again. All the curtains were partly drawn. She started to look around. The caravan was well equipped; two bedrooms, one with a double bed, the other with bunks; tiny shower room; tiny kitchenette, and living area. So far, so good. None of the other caravans appeared to be occupied. She had already checked that the warden's caravan was empty. She found duvets in a storage cupboard. She would have a dry night, even a warm night, tonight. She found that she could unlock the caravan door from the inside. She slipped out and connected the electricity supply. She would only use a little – just enough for a shower and a hot drink. She returned to the caravan, drew the curtains tightly, and unpacked her rucksack. She carried a sleeping bag, thermos flask, wash bag, two towels, two pairs of jeans, two shirts, a clean sweater, and two changes of underwear. She also had a primus stove, a small battery lamp, a torch, a lighter, a mug, small saucepan and a tin plate. She had a can of baked beans (with ring pull), half a loaf of bread, a small piece of cheese, six eggs, four tomatoes, half a cucumber, milk, and a handful of teabags. Riches indeed! Most important of all, in the outer pocket of the rucksack she had three biro pens and three fat A4 notepads.

She laid out the notepads and pens precisely on the central table. They would wait until tomorrow. Then she made a cup of tea, had a shower, and went to bed – on the double bed. What bliss! So tired, she slept soundly throughout the night, waking at dawn as usual. She slipped quietly down to the beach to watch the sun rise over the sea. Such clean, unadulterated beauty. Greedily, she absorbed it, as if starved. She had to take in as much as possible of everything that is beautiful in the world. In the distance she saw a fisherman wending his way down to the beach. Quickly and quietly she slipped back to the caravan. She did not want to be seen.

She boiled an egg, made toast and tea, using the little kitchenette. She cleaned up meticulously behind her.

Then she settled down with the notepads. She started to write. On she wrote, and on, all through the day, with an urgency. She was on a mission. She could not stop. Occasionally she stopped to think, but not for long. Then she started again – scribble, scribble, scribble, frantically. There was so much to get down, and she had so little time. She did not know how long she could stay in the caravan. Someone could come along at any time. As a matter of habit she kept her rucksack packed, ready for flight. She coughed. She had a nasty cough. She would stay here in the caravan as long as she could. She had enough provisions to see her through at least a week, and she would write and write and write. She smiled to herself. She had not planned to end up here. In fact, she had not planned anything at all, but this was perfect – as long as it lasted.

For several days, Josie continued in the same way, rising at dawn, going to the beach, and then scribbling and scribbling all day long. She coughed frequently. The food lasted. Her appetite was negligible, but she forced herself to eat something when she thought about it. She was getting weaker. One day she stopped writing, and looked at her hands. Holding them in front of her face, she examined them. They were like a labourer's hands, gnarled, brown, sinewy, knotted. She used to have such pretty hands. Then she looked in the mirror. Her face was brown, weatherbeaten, lined, worn, horrid! She used to be a beauty. "If this is old age" she thought "I want nothing of it". She went back to the notepad. She really did not feel very well. She would write a little longer, and then go to bed.

Madeleine and Tony were now only ten miles from

Brean. They thought it a good idea to stop at a pub and have lunch. There was a nice little pub just up the road. They pulled in. Glad of the cool interior of the pub, Madeleine ordered a large, cold white wine. Tony, a conscientious driver, ordered a pint of lime and soda. They were enjoying life. Having retired a couple of years ago, and finally got the children off their hands, they had bought a caravan, which they kept in Brean. They could get away whenever they liked and, hopefully, would eventually bring their grandchildren there for holidays. Not that any grandchildren had arrived yet. But they lived in hope. They ate at a leisurely pace. There was little to rush for these days, and life was kind. Their pensions were not fantastic, but adequate, provided they were careful. And there was always a little left for the things they enjoyed in life.

Back in the car again, they headed for the caravan at Brean. Madeleine had all the provisions in the boot. She was an organised sort of person, so Tony knew she would have catered for everything.

They arrived at the caravan. There was scarcely anyone else about. It was still early for the holiday season. Everything was in order, neat and tidy, as they had left it. Madeleine busied herself unloading the boot, whilst Tony opened the caravan door. As he opened the door, Tony recoiled, coughing, spluttering. Madeleine looked up, raced towards him. "What's the matter?" she cried. "Are you alright?". "I'm fine" he said. "It's the smell. It smells awful in there". He took his handkerchief out, "stay here" he said and, putting the handkerchief over his nose and mouth, he went in. Nothing seemed to be disturbed, but then he noticed the notepads and pens on the table.

Slowly he went through the caravan. Actually, he took only a minute but, to Madeleine, it felt like an hour. Tony emerged pale and gagging. He took the handkerchief from his face. "Don't go in there" he said, pulling out his mobile 'phone. He dialled 999. Madeleine and Tony waited in the car for the police to arrive.

The police arrived. The area was roped off. Suddenly the place was teeming with people. It's surprising how the locals get wind of any potential scandal; it's as if the jungle drums are out.

They found Josie lying, fully clothed, on the bed. There were no belongings anywhere, apart from the notepads. Everything else was neatly stashed in the rucksack. There was no food left, just teabags.

They searched the body. They found nothing to identify her; no cards, 'phone, bank details – nothing. Not even the labels on her clothes. They had all been cut out. There was a thin, worn wedding ring on her finger. She had on her a small worn purse with five pounds in it, but that is all.

Tony and Madeleine went to stay at a local bed and breakfast, where the landlady plied them with questions, which they could not answer, whilst, at the same time, pouring copious cups of tea. They felt they could not go home. It was all too upsetting, and they wanted to stay until all was resolved. Who was this poor lady? How had she ended up in their caravan? The landlady was kind and happily let them stay on.

After a week, a kindly policeman came to see them again. He told them the dead woman was Josie Murray. She had been a vagrant for the past several years; she was well known at shelters around the country. She never stayed anywhere more than a night or two, and then moved on. It appeared she had traversed the whole of England. She had seen a doctor in Exeter a couple of months ago. Apparently he had diagnosed cancer – severe – all the soft tissue. He had wanted her to go into a hospice where she would be cared for. But Josie refused, and disappeared. The last years of her life had been tough, but she was physically strong and, apart from the cancer, healthy. They could not yet trace any living relatives. Her notepads had, however, proved interesting. The police had kept them and were investigating the contents. They appeared to be genuine. When asked, the policeman, a kindly soul, thought it would do no harm if Tony and Madeleine were to be given a copy of what Josie had written. Kind people themselves, they were deeply affected by this tragic death in their own caravan. They felt that, if they could read what she had written, it might shine some light on this sad ending to her life.

Josie's notepad read..

"When I was a girl, I had such a charmed and exciting life. I was privileged beyond compare. My father was an officer in the diplomatic service. We lived overseas, in Africa. We were surrounded by servants. I had my own Ayah (African nanny). We were cared for, looked after. An only child, I had a tutor to teach me. My mother could not bear to send me back to boarding school in England, which was the fashionable thing to do in those days. We always lived in big houses with marble floors and wide, cool verandahs. My parents entertained frequently almost daily. I was acquainted with Kings, Princes, statesmen, governors, generals, admirals, scientists, authors, and so many more. Anybody who was anybody was entertained by my parents. I do not think that there were many famous people sixty-odd years ago whom I had not met.

As a child with blonde hair and blue eyes, I believe I was quite striking. I had learned at my mother's knee how to flirt with older gentlemen, and I think I was something of a favourite. Of course, we were taught manners in those days, and I knew how to behave. When nobody was about, I went wild but, as soon as guests arrived, I had to behave.

I spent the mornings with my tutor. I would then have lunch and a siesta, after which I was left to my own devices for a couple of hours. I would generally ask the syce to saddle up my pony, and ride out into the bush. I would ride out there for as long as I could, rounding up the wild animals, stampeding them, watching, observing. Galloping as fast as I could along the runway was a favourite pastime, or paddling up the luggers (river beds) when there was rain.

Then I would have to be at home, bathed and changed into a clean frock, white socks and sandals at 4.00 p.m. sharp for tea with Mother under the Baobab tree. The houseboy would bring out the silver tray with a lacey traycloth, and the silver teaset. There would always be cucumber or watercress sandwiches, scones with jam and cream, and cake. Sometimes I was late. I was not then popular. My mother was strict, and adhered to routine.

I remember my first ball. I was twelve years old. I had a new frock, and was so excited. The frock was baby blue taffeta, with a net overskirt, and a collage of pink rosebuds attached to a big blue sash around my waist, and cascading downwards. I had pink and blue ribbons in my hair. I knew how to dance, of course. I had been taught. Social graces were, in those days, considered to be an essential part of a girl's education. Every gentleman at the table danced with me. They had laid the dance floor out on the lawn. Whilst we danced in the balmy night air, we could hear the crickets and the bullfrogs out in the bush. It was all so wonderful – the band playing in their splendid uniforms, the tables decorated so prettily, the ladies in their ballgowns and makeup and perfume, and the gentlemen, all in white ties and tails. What made everything even more special were the twinkling lanterns and candles everywhere. Oh, how fine it all was! The food was wonderful; there were so many courses, I thought I would burst. And then there were the fireworks. I had never seen fireworks before. They were magic, just magic! My first ball. Nothing since has ever been quite as magical, carefree.

My life continued in much the same carefree way until I was eighteen. Then, the parents announced, I was to be sent off to Finishing School in Switzerland. I did not want to go. But the parents insisted, and off I flew to Switzerland. At first I was known as that "African" girl, but slowly I began to make friends, and enjoy my new life in Switzerland. In many ways it was different – so much more confined, so many rules "Thou shalt do this, thou shan't do that". We had to wear white gloves and hats when we went out, stockings and high heeled shoes – and the stocking seams had to be straight. So much restriction! And how I hated those uncomfortable suspenders. I had never had to wear stockings in Africa.

But there were lots of dances and balls in the evenings,

and so many dashing young men, many in uniform. We had such fun. One evening, when I was nineteen, a very handsome young man asked me to dance. I had not met him before, but he knew my friend, Alison, so I thought it was alright. He sparkled. His dark black curly hair bounced as he spoke to emphasise a point. He was animated, funny, witty. I fell head over heels in love. That was another wonderful evening!

A few days later I had the opportunity of asking Anthony (yes, that was his name) to a soiree at the Finishing School. I did not think he would accept, but he did and, after that, he asked me out to dinner. He took me right up into the Alps to a little Bistro weighted down by snow, but so warm and cosy inside with candles glowing everywhere and the smell of delicious food. It was so romantic. I suppose that was really the beginning of our relationship. Eighteen months later we were married. Anthony was English, and his parents insisted we would have to be married in England. They simply would not contemplate going to Africa for a wedding. Barbaric, they thought it. Instead, we went back to my home for our honeymoon, and I so love that continent. The honeymoon was ideal, bliss. We stayed for two months, but eventually Anthony said he had to get back to work.

Anthony was in publishing – newspapers, magazines. We lived in London, and it took me a long time to accustom myself to city life. I never quite knew what he did, but in those days wives were not expected to take much interest in their husbands' occupations. They were expected to stay at home, and be wonderful hostesses at all times. I found it a little difficult, after Africa, to have to do so many chores myself. We did have a maid and a cook, but it was not really enough. By and large, though, my life was good. I lunched with friends or with Anthony on most days, and we went out at least four evenings a week, to the theatre, concerts, dinner parties, sometime dances or balls. I cannot complain. I missed Africa, but that is to be expected. When I became pregnant, both Anthony and I were ecstatic. Herbert was born a year after we were married.

After Herbert, we could not have any more children, so we probably spoiled him. He was so precious to us. The years went by. My father died in Africa. My poor mother then came home to England, and bought a little cottage just outside Winchester. She never really settled. She was lonely on her own, and found it difficult to make friends. A couple of years after she came back to England we had a very cold winter; she contracted pneumonia, and died. I was sorry to lose her. We buried her in the village churchyard, under a beech tree. It was very bleak at the time, but I knew it would be pretty in the spring.

Herbert grew and grew. He was a happy boy with a delicious chuckle. He just loved life. One day we returned from a visit to the zoo by bus. We had had a wonderful time. Herbert chattered on and on about the bears, the lions, the monkeys, as any child would.

When we got to our stop, he jumped off the bus platform ahead of me. I turned to say "goodbye" to the conductor and, at that moment, my life collapsed. There was a screech of brakes. In his excitement, Herbert had hopped into the road. He probably never saw the car. He was killed outright. We buried him next to my mother, under the beech tree.

Anthony and I thought we would never emerge

from the hell we then entered. My own life was full of self-recrimination: "if only …", "if only I had watched him more carefully", "if only I had not spoken to the conductor". There were so many "if onlys".

The house was so quiet. When Anthony was at work, I found it unbearable. I took to walking. I walked and walked, all day long I walked, until Anthony came home, and I had to be there for him. He, himself, was becoming more and more morose. I did not pay much attention to him. Absorbed in my own grief, I felt he was equally absorbed in his.

We became distanced from each other. We stopped communicating. I still spent my days walking, and he seemed to spend more and more hours at the office.

One evening, Anthony said, at dinner "Darling, I've got some awful news". "What could be worse than what we've already been through?" I asked. "Whatever it is, Darling, we'll get through it". "You don't understand" he said "It'll be all over the papers tomorrow. I'm accused of fraud, of embezzlement. They're pressing for a trial". "But, Darling, you can't be. You'd never do anything like that" I cried. For a while he said nothing. Then, quietly "The trouble is, I don't know what I have been doing, or haven't been doing recently. Everything is a haze since Herbert died. I think I haven't been coping very well". I know I was crying. I gave him a big cuddle, but he was so quiet, so withdrawn. I poured him a brandy, but he would not drink it. Eventually he said "we'd better send Alice (our maid) out to get the papers tomorrow. If you don't mind, I think I'll go to bed now". I do not suppose he slept very well. He tossed and turned all night, and I certainly did not sleep at all.

The next morning, the papers were on the breakfast table. The things they said were foul. Anthony looked grey. He left for the office as usual, first holding me so tight I could not breathe. He kissed me and said "never forget, you are my life". I put my coat and hat on, and went walking again. I walked all day. When I returned, Alice told me there was a policeman waiting for me in the drawing room. I offered him tea. The policeman declined. He told me that, that morning, shortly after he had arrived at the office, Anthony had hanged himself. He had left a note. He handed it to me.

"My Own Darling" he wrote "As I told you this morning, you are my life. But I cannot stand the shame, the ignominy. I cannot face standing in the dock, and so I have decided to end it all. It seems that since Herbert died I have not been able to cope with anything. I love you so much, My Darling". I did not keep the note. The words are seared on my heart.

Anthony, too, was buried alongside my mother, with his son. Then there was all the furore of the press, meetings with lawyers, accountants. I did not understand much of what was going on. All I did understand was the agony I was in, and nobody seemed to notice. The staff left. Everything went: the house, the chattels. Everything had to be sold.

A few friends remained loyal, and they put me up, sometimes for months at a time. I continued in this way for four years until I thought their patience must have run out. I was still walking regularly. It was the only relief I had. I borrowed a rucksack from a friend, filled it with my basic requirements, and left. I have not seen anybody I then knew since. Nor do I want to. My life now is over.

I have been told I have not long to live. Good. I want to join my family again."

By time she finished reading, Madeleine was in tears. "How could such a lovely person end up like this" she said. Tony said "it's as if she was broken by life itself".

Tony and the policeman shuffled their feet, embarrassed by raw emotion. "Please, Darling, we've a little spare money. Can't we pay for her funeral – under the beech tree, with her family?" Madeleine asked. She blew her nose. Tony felt the police would be able to trace the location, now that they had her notepad. "Yes, of course we'll do it" he said.

Josie was buried under the beech tree alongside her mother, her husband, and her son. It was a bleak day, raining and windy. The vicar took the service, and, apart from a police officer, Madeleine and Tony were the only mourners there.

Shortly afterwards, Tony and Madeleine sold their caravan. They never went camping again.

THE GUIDE ROOM

It was breathtaking, absolutely beautiful! She had stopped on the brow of the hill, and there it lay before her, a gilded jewel set on a voluptuous green velvet pillow, all shimmering in the heat haze. Marjorie had heard so much about this house. It was stunning. There were lakes, fountains were playing merrily in the grounds. The estate was wonderfully planted, so many different species, and all complementing each other. It must have been designed by Capability Brown, she thought. There were trees everywhere; rich, luscious dark greens, lime, golden, silver. Sheep and cattle grazed contentedly. They were not hemmed in to fields, but wandered quietly over the estate.

The house itself had been built in 1650 (or at least started then). It had been built in just ten years. All that beautiful Bath stone, all that wonderful carving, all those windows. No builder these days could achieve so much in such a short space of time. She thought of how the stone was brought to the house, by horse and cart; she thought of the old tools they had used, the stonemasons chipping and carving away, all to create such glory. There must have been thousands of builders, craftsmen, stonemasons working to create this, she thought.

This golden house had nestled quietly here accommodating the same family for nearly four hundred years, avoiding civil wars, politics, conflict of any kind, probably because it was hidden in this secret valley. Had they not known where to look, few would have found it. The current Lord Pugh, the present incumbent, is the fourteenth direct descendant of the man who originally built this house.

Marjorie had applied for a job as a guide in the house. She had been accepted, given homework to do so that she would start the job with sufficient knowledge, and here she was, on her first day. A hundred and twenty-nine rooms, three hundred and fifty chimneys, and four hundred and sixteen windows, she remembered. Only twenty rooms were open to the public. Lord Pugh occupied one wing; offices another; archives occupied the top floor, another floor was for storage; nothing in these old houses was ever thrown away – four hundred years' of history, of things; most of the rest of the house was empty. She was excited.

The head guide, a bustling, busy person, ushered Marjorie into the Guide Room – the sacred precinct of the guides. She, herself, had an office which led off the guide room. The head guide was called Helen. There were several ladies and gentlemen sitting around the perimeter of the room, some in ancient armchairs, others on upright chairs. They all looked up. None spoke. "This is Marjorie, our newest guide" cheerfully Helen introduced her. "Hello", "Good morning". They were all very polite, and then went back to what they were doing. Helen introduced the guides. "This is Muriel, then we have Hermione, John, Gregory, Hazel, Jane, Melody, Susan, Janet, Simon, Francine, Bridget, and Ann. The others come in at different times". She smiled. "We have forty guides altogether. You'll get to know them soon enough". Marjorie wondered about that. How on earth would she ever remember all their names? "Now come with me into the office, and I'll brief you further". Marjorie was in a daze.

Once in the office, Helen purposefully closed the door. "I should warn you, some of the guides are a bit poisonous" she said. "I don't know why. Some of the newer ones have left because of them, but don't worry. If you have any problems, you can always speak to me, or to Ann. She's the assistant head guide. Takes my place when I'm off duty. We are open every day of the year except Christmas Day, and you will be expected to take your turn at weekends and on bank holidays. We are posting in all the rooms open to the public – twenty minutes in each room, then we move on. It's a good system. Nobody gets bored. Now, have you any questions?" Marjorie shook her head . "Good. You've done your homework. You know about all the rooms. But you may take your notes with you if you wish, until you're more confident. Now, we'd better start. The doors open in ten minutes".

They returned to the guide room. Helen was brisk. "Muriel in the drawing room, Hermione in the dining room, John in the Royal bedroom, Gregory in the blue library, Hazel in the green library, Jane in the music room" and so she went on until all the rooms were covered, except the state drawing room. "Marjorie, you follow Ann, and cover the state drawing room. Come along everyone. No slacking. The doors are opening".

"Don't forget, everybody" she called after them "Hang on to your radios at all times. Do NOT put them down, under any circumstances". And off they all trooped.

What a frantic rush everything was, and so much confusion! Marjorie, alone at last in the state drawing room, waiting for the public to arrive, marvelled at the exotic, opulent beauty of the place. It was a shame that the blinds were down, but they were down in all the rooms. The house archivist insisted on it – to preserve the treasures. An alarm went off. Marjorie had been warned about this. Sometimes members of the public would touch things, and set off the alarms. There was a call on the radio "Muriel in the drawing room. A baby has crawled under the ropes". There was an answering radio "Security here. We're on our way". Marjorie was terrified that she might have to use the radio herself. Gadgets worried her.

Two hours later, Marjorie found herself back in the Guide Room. "You've got fifteen minutes before you go out again" said Hermione, who had arrived ten minutes before Marjorie. So have your coffee now, whilst you've got the chance." "Where do I get the coffee?" asked Marjorie. "Oh, you bring your own, and your own mug and your own sandwiches". "Great" thought Marjorie, who had brought nothing, seems I'll lose a bit of weight today". She sat on one of the hard, upright chairs, and watched Hermione and Muriel tuck in to their respective lunch packs. Muriel got out a book,

Muriel was one of the older guides, set in her ways, and not (as Helen had assured Marjorie) particularly accurate in her knowledge of the house and its treasures, but she had been a guide for thirty years now, and nobody dared challenge her. Marjorie had already dubbed her "Madame Pince-nez". Muriel was aloof, arrogant. She did not speak to Marjorie at all, did not even look at her, and yet there were only three of them in the room. Marjorie took an instant dislike to her. She had already been warned that the one thing she must never do was to sit in Muriel's chair. Strictly speaking, she could sit in any chair, but Muriel had designated this chair for her own use many, many years ago, and nobody dared challenge her on it. It was more than their life was worth. The chair she was sitting on was uncomfortable; Marjorie went to sit down in a more comfortable armchair. "Oh no, dear" said Hermione "you can't sit there. That's Susan's chair. She'd be most upset". Marjorie went to sit in another chair. From behind her paperback, Muriel barked at her "Not there". She tried another chair. Third time lucky; "I think you could sit there for a while" said Hermione "until Jane comes back, but it's really her chair". Marjorie felt like Goldilocks in front of the three bears.

There was actually a problem with the chairs in the guide room. There were a few comfortable ones, but they were all "taken" by guides who had been there longest. The remaining hard-backed old dining chairs were singularly uncomfortable. Arranged round the room, like an old-fashioned dentist's waiting room, there were not enough of them. Sometimes the newer guides had to stand. One poor soul, who had upset Muriel on one occasion, was so terrified that, rather than enter the guide room, she sat on a bench outside during her breaks.

Hermione was elderly too, probably mid-eighties, but elegant, tidy. She dressed beautifully, and she was clearly well educated and erudite. Marjorie would come to learn that Hermione and Ann both spoke fluent French, and so took all the French tours round the house. Hermione was charming, one of the few guides to be kind to Marjorie. She showed her where things were. She always smiled a greeting, and she laughed a lot.

After fifteen minutes, Marjorie went out again "posting" they called it; talking to the public, telling them about the history of the house, the treasures. The next time she came back to the guide room, John and Gregory were there. They were both sweet, one a retired teacher, the other a retired vicar. They kept their heads down and did not get embroiled in the guide room politics, which Marjorie quickly discovered ran most guides' lives.

Gradually, Marjorie come to know which guide was which, although it was almost impossible to know them in the sociable sense. They were a very closed community, and she found it virtually impossible to break through. By and large, they were either retired, service wives, or gap year students.

Hazel, very short and sort of grey all over, was probably in her mid-forties. Her tongue was acid, and she was incredibly unfriendly towards Marjorie. She was very good with the public, though, when in the right mood. But, as Marjorie quickly discovered, she was a creature of moods. There could be long, sullen silences. Marjorie christened her "The grey dwarf". She always wore ridiculously high heels, consequently tottering around with her bottom sticking out behind her. Marjorie once asked Ann why

Hazel was so spiteful. "Oh, she's menopausal" Ann replied "and she's got man problems". "If I looked like her, and was so nasty, I'd have man problems too" said Marjorie. Ann, ever diplomatic, merely raised an eyebrow.

Jane and Susan were young graduates, filling their gap year. Jane was dumpy, intense, spotty. Downright ugly, actually, whereas Susan was very pretty, laughed a lot, and danced all over the place. Everyone loved Susan. "The sprite" Marjorie thought.

Janet was a strange fish. Arthritic, she limped heavily, one hip pushed out, bottom sticking out behind, shoulders leaning forward. Grey hair cropped short, she was almost bent double. Her conversation tended to be brief, sharp, staccato. She had been an officer in the army, and had married another officer. They were divorced now. She lived her life as if she was still in the army; discipline, rules, regulations. To her, the house and its contents were sacrosanct. She had become so attached to them that she guarded them jealously as if they were her own. One day Marjorie ventured from the room she was manning. No member of the public was about. She returned a script to the room she had just been in. Janet saw her. In a rage, wagging her finger in front of her, she limped as fast as she could down the long gallery towards Marjorie "That is a shooting offence. That is a firing squad offence" she railed. She was shouting, face red. Marjorie could not believe it. She giggled. Big mistake! "A shooting offence. Never leave your post. Never, never do that again, do you hear me?" raged Helen. She was apoplectic. "Hitler" Marjorie thought. She was incredulous, and found it very hard to keep a straight face.

Simon was young, laid back, working here because

it was something to do, but did not really know what he wanted from life. What he really wanted was to travel, just travel. He had already been round the world once. Now he wanted to go again. Living at home with his long-suffering parents, he was saving up, so that he could be off again.

Francine, breezy, mad as a march hare, spoke fluent French, so was useful to the house. But actually she was a liability, or so Helen thought. Her mind was all over the place, and she was SO forgetful. She frequently got her shifts muddled up, came in when she was supposed to be off duty, and did not come in when she was supposed to. A lovely lady, she laughed a lot, asked your name every time she saw you. She had been a guide for years, but she still asked the names of even the oldest serving guides. "I do forget names, you see" she would say, and then, charmingly, ask again. In the guide room she chattered endlessly about all manner of inconsequential things.

Bridget was German, married to an Englishman. Her style was Teutonic. She conducted the German speaking tours. But if the slightest thing unusual happened, she simply could not cope. She panicked and, flustered, made everything much worse. Her biggest problem was that she could not laugh at herself. Everything had to be analysed in the minutest detail. One day Susan told her there were two transvestites wearing outsize tartan kilts and large red wigs and red noses going round the house. They were, in fact, thieves and about to try and steal a famous painting. Poor Bridget got into a terrible stew. She immediately called the security guards who told her they were on to it, to wait for the men to arrive, and when they got there, to contact security again, but not to alarm them in any way.

Bridget spent the whole of the next half hour agonising over these two men, waiting for them, looking for them. But they did not appear. When, eventually, the security men told her it was a practical joke, she could not see the funny side at all. She was furious, and felt she had been made a fool of.

Melody was fun. She simply did the job to prevent herself from getting too bored. At home all day, children grown up, and husband at work, she had a daily help and a gardener and no hobbies. She might as well do this. Marjorie liked Melody instinctively.

Melody hated Muriel – had a vendetta against her. Muriel had once been intolerably rude to Melody and had refused to apologise. "If ever she speaks to me again" said Melody "I swear I'll knock her bloody false teeth out".

One day Marjorie asked Melody "why is Helen so uptight about the radios?". Melody laughed and whispered. "Last month, when Helen was posting, she put her radio down on her stool whilst talking to someone. A young lad pinched it. He waited until he was outside the building, then sent all sorts of messages over the system. There was a fire in the library; everybody in wheelchairs had to get out of them and walk, and so on. It caused chaos!" Melody giggled conspiratorially. "And, of course, Helen, head guide, had egg all over her face. So, you see, she's very sensitive now about the radios".

An hour later, Marjorie found Melody on her hands and knees beside a radiator, scrabbling around behind it. "What are you doing?" she asked. "I've lost my bloody radio" she said. "Would you believe it, just after I told you why Helen's so uptight about them. I dropped it down behind the radiator, and I can't get it back. Helen'll sack me for this" she moaned. "Can you see if you can find Steve (one of the security men). It'll need a stick to poke this thing out. But for God's sake be discreet. I don't want to be caught". Marjorie found Steve who obligingly came to the rescue. Melody fluttered her eyelids at him. "Oh, he's gorgeous" she breathed. "I'd have him any night". Melody had a bit of a crush on Steve.

What Marjorie found most disturbing was the way in which, once in the Guide Room, those guides present would discuss, and verbally tear limb from limb all the other guides. They were venomous. Should one of those being discussed return, all was sweetness and light. Such hypocrisy! Another trait many of them had was their habit of name dropping. "Oh, I said to Lady Pish Posh only the other day"; "my cousin works for the Queen Mother, you know, and she knows everything that goes on there. Everything" said with raised eyes, and dripping with hidden innuendo. "Of course, I know all Lord Pugh's secrets, but I can't possibly divulge!" What sad old bitches they are, thought Marjorie. They've got no life of their own, so have to live through the lives of others.

As Marjorie discovered over the following months, life at the house was a series of little cameo events, all linked by unseen threads . Many of the guides were incredibly set in their ways, and wholly unable to cope with even the tiniest disruption to their own routines. With so many individual routines to contend with, life in the house was sometimes hilarious.

All the guides were warned there would be a fire alarm practice during the ensuing days. The house steward took any potential threats to the house very seriously, and the estate office had received several over the past few months.

When the alarm eventually did go off, Marjorie jumped out of her skin. So did all the public. The guides' duty was to get all the public out of the house, and off on to a grassy bank nearby as quickly and efficiently as possible. Wheelchairs were a particular problem, especially when on the first floor.

Marjorie shut the doors of the room she was in, and herded her charges towards the designated exit. The wheelchairs were sent to the top of the stairs where they would be met by security staff and taken out. Apparently the occupants of the chairs were expected to get out of them and walk down the stairs in an emergency. The banisters were wide. Perhaps they could slide down, thought Marjorie. Her charges were helpful and obliging, and she got them all out of the house within two minutes. So far so good! But then she had to get them over on to the grass verge. Once outside, however, they had lost all sense of urgency. They sauntered along, Marjorie shepherding as fast as she could. She took over a baby buggy and a large shoulder bag from one woman who was also holding another child, whilst her husband was trying to prevent the two large hot coffees he was carrying from spilling over. God, what are his priorities?! Marjorie thought. She told him to put the coffees down; he could come back for them later. Suddenly Marjorie was aware of long-legged Hazel tearing past her at an incredible pace. "Come on, Marjorie" she yelled. We've got to get to the grass verge and report in. Come on. Run. Hurry up". And she raced on. Marjorie looked around her. Hazel had outstripped all the members of the public, effectively abandoning them. Well, there it was. Cool, self-contained Hazel in a complete tizz, and out of control. "Fat lot of good she is" thought Marjorie as she struggled with the buggy and the bag. She got to the rallying point, complete with all her charges, and within the time frame allocated. She breathed a large sigh of relief.

Janet (Hitler) always had to sit in the same chair in the guide room, at the same table. She would always get out her picnic things, Lay a table napkin perfectly square on the table in front of her, set her plate, knife and fork exactly as on a dining room table, and her coffee mug. She would then sit back, sigh, and open her lunch box. She would spoon the contents on to her plate, reposition her knife and her mug so that they were perfectly aligned, before she began to eat. She ate slowly, without talking. If Marjorie listened, she could hear Janet masticating.

Hermione, on the other hand, would bring in a little box of sandwiches, which she always ate standing, chattering nineteen to the dozen to anyone who would listen. She gulped her hot coffee in between sentences. Everyone loved her. She showed interest in all the other guides, never forgetting to ask after their mother, husband, child, whomever they might be having a problem with.

The grey dwarf was on a permanent diet. She ate lettuce leaves – by the hundreds. And carrots. Nothing else, as far as Marjorie could ascertain. Convinced she would turn into a rabbit, Marjorie was waiting for her ears to grow. She wore big gypsy earrings. "What are you looking at?" she snapped at Marjorie. "Oh, nothing, just thinking" she said. The silly little woman did look ridiculous. Her heels were six inches high - platform shoes. She tottered on them. She certainly could not walk.

Janet had been to the "Ladies". She returned to the

Guide Room and headed off into the house to "post". As she passed, people giggled and smirked at her. Janet glowered. She really did not like the public. She would have been far happier if all these lovely treasures were kept away from them. They did not appreciate what they saw, anyway. They were all ignorant. All those people were whispering behind her back. How rude! She stomped along, apparently oblivious. Ann, looking across the Great Hall, saw Janet. She could not believe what she saw. It would do Janet good to come down a peg or two, she thought. She bossed and bullied the public, treating them really badly. She might have been knowledgeable, but she was an awful guide. Janet's skirt was hitched up at the back into her knickers – big bloomer things. Her tights were all wrinkly at the back of the knee. Ann smirked and left her to it. It was not like Ann to be malicious, but she really had had enough of Janet.

One morning, everyone was in the guide room, being briefed as to where they were posting that day, when Francine rushed in. late as ever. At least she was there, thought Marjorie. Francine frequently did not appear at all. Breathless, dishevelled, mouthing apologies, poor Francine was her usual disorganised self. Helen gently steered her towards the office, where she had a word. Francine's blouse was inside out, the buttons undone, except two, which were the wrong ones anyway. She had one black shoe on and one brown, and her hair was all over the place. Later, Helen was heard to say wearily "She's such a lovely lady, but I really think the time has come to let her go. She doesn't seem to be aware of the world around her any more". "How old is she?" asked Marjorie. "Oh, she's only seventy-eight, but she's had a lot of problems with her daughter – has to look after the grandchildren all the time, and finds it very difficult. I think that and guiding at this house is all too much for her". Quietly it was suggested to Francine that she should have a rest from guiding whilst looking after her grandchildren. Helen was a kind soul, and Francine never realized that, in fact, she was getting the sack.

"The thing about guiding", said Helen to Marjorie "is that anyone can do it, regardless of age. So we have a lot of pensioners here, supplementing their pensions. Some do it because they are bored, but others do it because they really need the income. We have six octogenarians working as guides. They're very good. But they do creak a lot, and those who have been here a long time think they know it all, but they are not historically accurate, and it's hard to persuade them to change. I worry about the creakers; there are a lot of stairs, and they're up and down them all day". "That's rich" thought Marjorie. She had already noticed that Helen, herself, had an arthritic hip and walked with a far more noticeable limp towards the end of the day. Helen was, nonetheless brisk and sprightly, but Marjorie thought she would have been in considerable pain. "The first thing John does when I get in" said Helen "is to pour me a stiff whisky. And I won't do anything until I've had that. Then I can start again". "I should think you bloody well need it" thought Marjorie. Being head guide was physically very demanding; on your feet all day long, up and down stairs, always on the go. Helen scarcely ever had a moment even to eat her sandwiches at lunchtime.

One day, posting in the children's room, a lady with two children approached Marjorie. "Who is that little girl in the corner over there?" she asked. Marjorie looked. "What little girl?" The woman's son said "oh, don't pay any attention to Mum. She's a psychic – sees people all over the place". "There's a little girl there, about ten years old" said the woman. "She's got blonde hair, blue eyes. Her hair's dressed in ringlets – probably Victorian. And there are so many dogs in this room. Actually I'm seeing dogs all over the house. There are greyhounds, King Charles spaniels. Oh, lots more! Don't mind me" she laughed. "I'm always seeing things. Come on children". And off they went. Marjorie peered into the corner where the child was supposed to be – nothing. She spent the rest of her shift peering about, looking over her shoulder, looking for ghosts. But she never saw anything. Once back in the guide room, she told Ann what had happened. "Oh" said Ann "That would be Geraldine. She died from consumption round about 1810. She was eleven years old". "There are lots of ghosts here. I've seen some, but Muriel's seen the most. She sees them almost daily". It was now autumn. By four o'clock in the afternoon the rooms were beginning to get really dark and gloomy. In case of fire, the guides were not allowed to turn the lights on, so lighting in the house was minimal. Marjorie was very conscious of the fact that, even when totally alone, she was surrounded by people, but she could never see them. How disappointing! She was longing to see a ghost. The atmosphere in the house was always warm, welcoming. She never felt frightened, just frustrated that she could not see all her companions.

As Marjorie became more familiar with the procedures, the house, her fellow guides, she became more aware of the pettinesses, the rules, the small-mindedness of the place. Each guide had to clock in with a card, was issued with a pass number which had to be tapped out on each door they passed through. They had to raise a tab on a board to say whether they were in the house or not. They also had to make a written entry of their time of arrival and of leaving. They had to collect their guide badge and sign for it, signing again at the end of the day when they returned it. When they took wheelchairs up in the lift they had to put up a tab in the lift, which indicated the number of wheelchairs on any given floor at any given time, and again when they took the wheelchairs down. Woe betide anyone who forgot to do any of these things. A lot of it was health and safety stuff, but none the less onerous for that. Once in the house, even in their breaks, they were not supposed to leave it, so some of the guides told Marjorie. "To hell with that" thought Marjorie, who craved fresh air. She went outside during her breaks – just to get some fresh air. The house, huge as it was, got very fuggy with all the windows closed and some two thousand people a day passing through it. Putty faced Jane and Susan the sprite. were aghast at her audacity. Marjorie would have expected Susan to have more spirit.

Marjorie was told off for not sitting on her stool in a particular and precise spot; she had moved it a few inches so that she could see out of the window. She was told off for talking too long to enthusiastic members of the public, and again, for not speaking enough to them; she was told off for not having an adequate dress sense. She had worn a bomber jacket in to work. She was told off for leaving her mug on the draining board after she had washed it up. She was told off for walking grass in to the house on the soles of her shoes. She was told off for spilling yoghurt on to the guide room carpet (she had never eaten yoghurt in the guide room). And it was not just Helen, the head guide, who told her off, but any of the other guides, who felt it their right to chastise newcomers for the slightest misdemeanour. One day she tripped and, reaching out to steady herself, was told off for attempting to touch the furniture. "Don't touch" screamed a horrified Bridget. If a child reached out to touch something, whether they did touch or not, Bridget would shout in stentorian tone "Don't touch". Occasionally the parents retaliated. She was unapologetic.

Lord Pugh, himself, was a strange character. He wore colourful, ethnic clothes most of the time, wore his hair long, and wandered around the house barefoot. By and large, he rattled around in this great house all on his own. Frequently he interspersed with the public, chatting to them as he went. Once they realised who he was, they were delighted. His Lordship, for all his reputation as a roistering party-goer/giver, was a sad and lonely man, and mixed with the public just for the company. He was always hospitable, polite, charming and courteous. His wife had left him, and his children had grown up and left home. One day, of course, his son would inherit the house. Then the whole caboodle would be his responsibility. He frequently had luncheon parties at the house. "I bet he's got a fantastic wine cellar" said Marjorie. "Oh no" said Muriel. "He buys only the cheapest plonk he can get. He's very tight with money."

Most of the people working in the house were incredibly loyal to him. Marjorie found it touching. His house steward, his house-keeper, cook, cleaners, security staff, guides – all loved him as much for his weaknesses, it seemed, as for his strengths. It was their duty to protect him, his family, his house, it's treasures, and his reputation. They nearly all lived in cottages on the estate, paying modest rents. The cottages were neat, clean, tidy, with lovely old English gardens. The setting was idyllic. It was exactly like the mediaeval system of fealty to the Lord of the Manor, thought Marjorie. But it seemed to work.

The summer progressed (the job was seasonal), and during July and August, the hours got longer and longer; the hoardes trudging through the house grew larger and larger. It meant the guides had to be ever more vigilant in ensuring no treasures were touched, broken, stolen. The house became more and more stuffy and airless, but somehow the guides survived. Marjorie's initial enthusiasm for the job was beginning to pale. She minded so much the lack of fresh air, and consequently got very tired each day. Guides were not paid well. She felt that she would see the season through, but not return next year.

Eventually it was the last day of the season for all but a handful of guides who worked the year through. After a particularly tiring posting, Marjorie returned to the guide room, to find only Gregory was there. "This is it, Gregory" she said. "My last day, and at last I'm going to make an impact". She rushed around the room moving all the chairs into different positions. Gregory, silent at first, chuckled, and then joined in. "I've wanted to do this for years" he said, puffing happily. It took them less than five minutes to move all the chairs into completely different places, and still nobody else came in. "Quick, let's get out of here" she said. They scuttled out, down to the guide exit. As they walked towards the car park Gregory shook Marjorie firmly by the hand. "All the best" he said, "And thank-you for bringing some laughter into the house. I shall miss you".

The house, however, had cast its spell on Marjorie, as it did on everyone. She still returns regularly to visit it, maybe to walk in the grounds, maybe to just sit and stare, or maybe to go inside and marvel at the treasures within. She always feels calm and content when she is there, no matter what else is going on in the world. And in all such places, where there are so many staff, and such an eclectic mix of people, there will be pettinesses, differences. But there is also so much care, laughter and humour, kindness, love even. It's a mixed bag, and what makes society rich. After all, the house had survived for nigh on four hundred years, and will undoubtedly survive for another four hundred years. The house is alive.

MALLOW

It's done. Today I killed my dearest friend.

Mallow and I have been together, through thick and thin, for thirteen years. My daughter and I chose her when she was a tiny little bundle, just six weeks old. She was chubby, fat little knees and great big paws, floppy ears, a solid little dog. Even her cheeks were chubby. She was so chubby, she could scarcely waddle over to us, tiny tail wagging furiously. Already her face had the marvellous black and tan markings of the true German Shepherd. We did not choose her. She chose us. Scrambling over the side of the puppy box, she followed us down the garden. She was not yet very steady on her feet, and, trying to run, fell over. Somehow her back legs got in front of her front legs. But that was Mallow. Always so enthusiastic!

Two weeks later, we were allowed to collect her. She was now eight weeks old. This tiny, solid ball of fluff threw up in the car on the way home. We did not mind.

She was clearly miserable in the car. I would have to accustom her to it gradually. When we arrived at home, my son was waiting excitedly. He had prepared a little food bowl, water bowl, bed and toys. This was going to be a very spoiled little puppy. She had a very posh long kennel club name, Jadzeah Delglish of Chairn. We could not use any part of that, so the first thing to do was to give her a name. We had a family conference, and my daughter said "She's as soft as marshmallow". That was it; we called her "Marshmallow", "Mallow" for short. Mallow was lying, fast asleep, at our feet, tummy full. She was content.

We already had a little mongrel called "Lucky" because he was lucky to be alive. Lucky and Mallow got on well. And Lucky no doubt taught Mallow a few tricks. By the time Mallow arrived Lucky was eight years old. Mallow, soon to grow into a great big dog, quickly became the pivotal focus of the whole household. She was endearing, affectionate, intelligent. She learned everything we taught her so quickly. Whilst teething, she was pretty destructive; all the books pulled out of the bookcase, and half chewed; all the childrens' videos and tapes chewed; table legs, chair legs, all things leather. But it was only a phase, and every puppy chews. We simply had to live through it.

We lived in the country. She had such fun. Wherever Mallow went, Lucky followed. A timid little dog, he lacked Mallow's adventurous spirit. Whereas she was as bright as a button, we had long since concluded that poor little Lucky had only a pea-sized brain. One day, I found the 'fridge door open and a whole chicken missing. Mallow had learned how to open the 'fridge. We had to put a child lock on it. We were out one day, and left her in the house. When we returned a policewoman was waiting in our drive. Lucky was waiting in the kitchen. Mallow had discovered how to open the windows, had hopped out and was chasing Roe deer through a field full of sheep when spotted by the policewoman in a patrol car. She brought Mallow home. I was sincerely grateful to her. Fortunately Mallow's attention was centred on the deer. Had she chased the sheep, the farmer would have shot her, as was his right. I knew Mallow would never be able to catch the deer, and would do them no harm, but I was terrified she would get out again and be shot. So all the window catches were changed.

I had a wonderful little four-seater cabriolet. When the children were with me, Mallow would sit upright in the back, grinning from ear to ear. When the children were not with me, she sat in the front passenger seat, looking for all the world as if she owned the car, and I was the chauffeur. Her ruff was growing, and she was becoming more and more handsome - a good looking teenager. She attracted a lot of admiring glances.

The most extraordinary thing about her was the bond which formed between us. It was as if she could read my mind. When I was at work, she always knew when I was due home, and she would be waiting at the front door fifteen minutes before I drove in to the drive, no matter what time of day it was. She knew when I needed company, when I wanted to be alone. She knew all my moods. And she was always welcoming, affectionate, no matter how bad a temper I was in. She loved classical music – not pop. She particularly loved anyone playing the piano. She would lie underneath it, tongue lolling, smiling happily.

Mallow was happiest when the whole family was together. Should one of the children be out at night, she would keep watch by the front door until they returned. When out walking, she would herd us up together, rounding up any stragglers.

We moved house five times during her lifetime. She never complained, but took it all in her stride. The children grew up, went off to university, and Mallow, Lucky and I were left alone for the greater part of the time. We moved to Kingston upon Thames.

By now Mallow was fully grown. A magnificent dog, resplendent mane, long glossy coat, she had the sweetest temperament. Gentleness personified, she was frequently attacked by other dogs. She was a favourite target of feisty little terriers. She would never retaliate, but shake them off gently. On one occasion, she trotted along the path with a tiny Jack Russel clinging to her mane, its little legs swinging. It was determined not to let go. The only occasion in her life when she retaliated was when she was attacked by a particularly fierce and very large mongrel – part Rottweiler, my daughter told me. That animal meant business. Within seconds, Mallow's underbelly was deeply slashed. She retaliated. The fight was fierce, but Mallow won. Bloodied and bowed, the mongrel ran off. It's owner screamed that she would sue for damages. Mallow smiled. She was a bit of a mess, but it mostly cleaned off. She did need some stitches.

Mallow was beautiful and intelligent, and her temperament so sound, that I decided we should breed from her. She was a bit off colour the day I had arranged to take her to the vet, to be hip-scored. In fact, she had been a bit off colour for the past few days. It was nothing one could put one's finger on, but I thought I would mention it to the vet. The vet said "This dog has to be operated on immediately". "What?" I said. "If she's not operated on within the next twenty-four hours" she said "she'll die. See here", and she showed me her stomach, "she's got a pyrametra. It's a big one, and it's got to come out. She's severely dehydrated. We'll have to rehydrate her first, and then operate. She's too weak at the moment". "She always has plenty of water" I stuttered. "What is a pyrametra anyway?" "She probably hasn't been feeling well enough to drink," she said. Has she been off her food at all?" "Not noticeably." "A pyrametra is a cancerous growth in the uterus. I may have to do an hysterectomy".

The following forty-eight hours were awful. Why had I not realized how sick Mallow was? I felt guilty. She could not have puppies now. How would I tell the children? Please God, let her survive this. Get her through it. Two days later, Mallow came home. She was weak and groggy, but otherwise alright. The vet said she was lucky to be alive; the tumour had been the size of a grapefruit and, unfortunately, he had no choice but to remove the womb. I sent the vet an effusive thank-you note with the cheque.

We loved walking in Richmond Park. Mallow would run ahead, and Lucky would trail along behind. One day, walking along a narrow path through the tall ferns, we rounded a bend and there, in front of us were two Red deer – hinds. They were facing us, and very obviously meant business. They are big creatures, and quite capable of doing serious damage, even killing. They were only twenty yards away. I yelled at the dogs and ran for my life. The dogs followed. But I knew I could not outstrip the deer. I turned to see them gaining on me rapidly. They would bring me down, no doubt. Then Mallow suddenly turned, faced the deer, ran towards them and turned again. It was a very deliberate act. She drew them off, away from me. One of the hinds caught up with her, and knocked her down. As she rolled over and over on the ground, the hind pounded at her spine with her hooves. I screamed at Mallow "Run, Mallow, run", Somehow she recovered, got up and ran. She escaped battered and bruised, but intact. It was not the fault of the deer; they had babies hidden in the ferns which we could not see. But they have been known to kill several dogs, and sometimes even people, by that pounding on the spine. Instinctively they are trying to break it. From their perspective, they were protecting their babies.

On another occasion in the park, my daughter and I were out with the dogs in the autumn. Evening was drawing on, and darkness came rapidly. We were still in the middle of the park. We could hear the stags rutting all around us. They sound particularly scary in the dark. Then we became aware that there were two stags baying at each other, and we were directly between the two. Should one of them charge, and we were in the way – we could not even contemplate the consequences. We did not have to call the dogs. They knew the danger. They kept very close to us, tails and heads down, as we hurried towards the gate.

Above all else, Mallow loved swimming. Living in Kingston was ideal for her; she had the Thames and the lakes in the park. People would throw their hands up in horror when they saw her and say "Oh, she'll get Veills disease" but she never did. She was a strong swimmer. She did frighten me on one occasion. She ran, as was her wont, straight towards the river and, delightedly, plunged in. What she had not realized was that the tide was out, and so when she jumped, there was a five foot drop. She sank down under the water and seemed to take ages to come back up. She started swimming against the current. The tide was coming in. It was a hard swim. There were boats moored all along the bank. And the sides of the bank were at least six feet high. She could not get back to land. Her only chance of getting out of the water was to swim until we found a slope where she could get out. She had to swim in the middle of the river, outside the moored boats. I ran along the river bank with her, shouting encouragement. There was nobody aboard any of the boats. About two miles further on, she was weakening; we were nearly in Twickenham, and still nowhere to get her out. She had to swim on. Eventually we came to a spot where there was a very steep slope. I tried to get down to help haul her out of the water, but my feet slipped out from under me. My shoes had leather soles. Then two teenagers came running up. They had seen what was happening. In a trice, they had slithered down the bank to the water's edge, hauled Mallow out of the water (in itself, a considerable feat; she weighed four and a half stone, even when dry. With a coat full of water, it would have been more). They helped her struggle up the bank, and before I could thank them properly, they had disappeared. Within a couple of minutes Mallow had recovered sufficiently to be able to walk home. I shall be eternally grateful to those dear boys.

It is my belief that we get out of life as much as we put into it. Mallow had saved my life in the park, and now her life was saved in return, in the river. I have had German Shepherds all my life, and every one has been special. I do not know what it is about this particular breed of dog which creates such a bond with human beings. Is it their intelligence? Is it their courage, their loyalty, their sense of guardianship? They do need to be handled properly. Not for the faint-hearted, owners should not take them on unless they know what they are doing. They need to be kept occupied, they need space. Boredom, for them is a problem. They need kindly control. It is no use shouting at a German Shepherd, or beating it. They have long memories. Once you have owned and bonded with one, no other dog will do.

Sometimes I would take her to the south coast, and we would swim side by side out to sea. Lucky would sit, melancholy, on the beach, waiting for our return. It must have been quite frightening for him. He was only little, and would not have been able to see us over the waves.

I cannot stress too highly Mallow's sense of guardianship. My son swears she saved him from being attacked by muggers whilst out walking with her. My daughter always felt safe when she had Mallow with her, as, indeed, I did. At night, Mallow would lie at the top of the stairs where she could keep an eye on what was going on down below, and guard the family as we slept. My son came home late from a party one night. Somewhat the worse for wear, he was wearing a party mask. He placed a foot on the bottom stair, and froze. All he could hear was that deep, dark, back of the throat growl. He did not dare move. Pulling off his mask "Mallow, it's me" he cried. Immediately, she jumped up, tail wagging. My large and extended family all knew where we kept the door key. But, without exception, they tell the same tale. When we were out, they could get in to the house. Mallow would always let them in. But then they were halted in their tracks and did not dare move. It was always the same. Mallow would sit politely in front of them, but she was growling in the back of her throat. It is a blood curdling sound. We were never burgled.

Mallow was by now becoming arthritic. I expected it. German Shepherds are prone to it. She was still able to come out on our long rambling walks, but had to rest frequently. Her spirit was so willing, but the flesh was getting progressively weaker. We did all we could to make her life more comfortable, but in this last year she went downhill rapidly. The summer was particularly hot, thirty degrees, and she suffered dreadfully. By now she was on steroids – just to relieve the pain. They made little difference. The heat made it worse. I cut all her coat off. She looked terrible. My once noble beauty was reduced to a little teddy bear of a creature with a massive proud head. But, rather like myself, I felt the time had come when comfort had to take precedence over appearance. She could no longer go up and down stairs unaided. She could walk no more than ten yards without collapsing. Even getting up and sitting or lying down were painful. Every moment of every day she was in pain. The time had come.

We went to the vet, a particularly kind man. Mallow put up her last resistance. She did not want to go into that veterinary surgery. She came, nonetheless. As she lay on the floor, I produced a sausage from my handbag. It was a very special sausage – wild boar and cranberry. Mallow had not lost her interest in food. She turned towards the sausage, ears pricked, taking a piece gently from my hand as the vet slid the needle in to her leg. She swallowed the sausage, smiled at me, snored, and she was gone.

I stood up. She will know no more pain. There she lay on the floor, somehow very small and crumpled. My dearest, my darling friend!

At that moment there was an enormous clap of thunder. We all jumped. It had been a lovely summer's day, mid August. The heavens opened. We were treated to torrential rainfall, thunder, lightning, huge hailstones. It lasted some ten minutes. The gods were giving Mallow a right royal send off. And then the sun came out again.

THE MISOGYNISTS

Andy was introducing Gavin. Andy was the Regional Manager, and Gavin was to be the new Office Manager. "Gavin is going to be a GREAT manager. We are very lucky to have him. You have no idea how hard I have worked to get him here. He's one of the best salesmen in the business" he announced. (In the insurance industry Managers are frequently expected to sell as well as to manage the branch). He introduced Gavin to each consultant individually. "How do you do". They shook hands. He moved on.

Andy was balding, a nonentity really. Nobody knew how he had got the job of Regional Manager. He did have the gift of the gab, so had probably been a good salesman.

There was a strange phenomenon throughout the industry. It is said that Managers only promote those who are not as good as themselves at the job. In other words, they are terrified of promoting someone who might be better than they are, thus losing them their own job. It applies even today, but in those days it was far worse. Hence, barrow boys, anyone who could sell, could be promoted to management, regardless of their managerial skills or abilities. It was considered sufficient that they knew how to sell (ergo they would be able to teach others to sell). It did not always follow. And many who would have been brilliant managers were ignored.

This was the insurance industry in the eighties. The Consultants, all self-employed, were a mixed bag. Ted, a cockney, was waiting to retire. Ted was conscientious, knowledgeable, a kindly man. Having been in the business for many years, he had a regular clientele and made a reasonable income, sufficient for his needs. Aziz, proud to call himself Persian, was a bachelor. Ambitious, he was quiet, thoughtful, analytical, and highly intelligent. Aziz would have made a brilliant manager, but he was too clever for his own good, and was consequently always overlooked. Padraig, the Irishman, was a wag – full of fun and laughter, telling jokes by the score. He was well-educated, intelligent and sensitive, loved by everyone he met. Molly was Glaswegian, dark-haired, feisty. It was sometimes difficult to understand what she was saying, her accent was very thick. Garth was a cheeky East Ender who had just joined the company. He had no prior experience of the industry. He had been a carpenter. Eleanor, a single Mum, educated, spoke as if she had a plum in her mouth, and Bill, a larger than life ex Salvation Army Preacher, was not the brightest button, but would never hurt a fly. Then there was Ann, the office administrator, and Jane, her assistant. Ann and Jane ran the office; they were responsible for all the paperwork, answering telephone calls when consultants were out, and the general smooth running of the office. They did a sterling job, and were appreciated for their efforts.

Molly, Ted, Aziz and Bill, between them, had been in the industry for over seventy years. They had a wealth of knowledge to pass on to the others.

Gavin was not tall, about 5'8". He had glittering brown eyes and a funny little chin, which looked as if it had been squashed. His thick black hair was slicked back and well greased. "Looks like a bloody spiv" thought Eleanor. "Oh God, not another one" thought Padraig. "Och, he's awful" thought Molly, and "I wonder how long he'll last" thought Aziz. Ted was weary, and did not bother to speculate about the man at all, and Bill thought "I'd better get on the good side of him, then".

After the introductions and murmured solicitudes, Andy said "Well, I think we can all go across the road now. Drinks are on me". And off they all trooped to the pub. This had become a lunchtime ritual. The girls would have a couple of glasses of wine each, the men a couple of beers or, in Padraig's case, Guinness, and Aziz would sometimes have a glass of wine rather than beer. It was a necessary kind of bonding. The industry was hard. They had to live on their wits, never knowing whether they would bring income home or not.

For every client who did business with them on which they were paid commission, there were several who did not do business. Sometimes they would put hours of hard work into an individual, only to be rejected, and they went away empty-handed. Then there were those clients who had done business (investments, savings schemes, insurance policies, pensions), and, for whatever reason had reneged on the deal or simply stopped the scheme – regular saving, insurance premiums, or pension, in which case all commissions already paid to the consultant would be clawed back by the company. They dreaded the clawbacks. Being paid monthly in arrears, inevitably, as soon as they got it, the money had gone – bills, mortgage payments, children, clothes, food – all the usual things which people spend money on. If one of them had earned £2,000 one month and it was clawed back the next – it was virtually impossible to pay back, so it would be withheld from the following month's pay. It meant that consultants frequently found themselves with absolutely no income for several months at a time. But they still had their regular commitments, bills to pay. Life was hard, and camaraderie was essential to survival.

Eleanor was good at getting information out of people without their realizing that they were being quizzed. She sat down next to Gavin. "So, Gavin" she smiled "tell me about yourself". Aziz, Padraig, Garth and Molly gathered round Andy. It was important to stay in favour with him, after all, and Ted sat a little apart with Ann and Jane.

It was a Friday lunchtime. Andy knew that they all avoided client appointments on a Friday afternoon, which was why he had chosen that time to introduce Gavin to them.

Friday afternoons were for unwinding. This Friday, with Andy's encouragement, they stayed in the pub all afternoon. Ann and Jane went back to the office to man the 'phones, but the others stayed on. They all drank too much, irrespective of the fact that they had to drive home afterwards. As they said their good-byes they were wondering what the next few weeks would be like. The branch manager in that industry made a huge impact on the running of the office, the ambience, the atmosphere, and Eleanor had established that Gavin had been no more than a double glazing salesman before he joined their company. He knew nothing about the insurance industry or about man management. "Ye Gods in Heaven" said Padraig "what is he going to bring to the party? Now we're being managed by a barrow boy. "

The following week, Gavin was embarrassingly craven in Eleanor's presence. Eleanor was one of the consistent high fliers in the office; she had done particularly well that month. Gavin knew he had to back the high fliers. They were the ones who would bring him his bonuses. Actually, Aziz, Padraig, Eleanor, and Bill all managed to do well throughout the year. It was largely because they ran seminars; they invited upwards of a thousand people at a time. On average, they would get a four percent turnout. It was hard work to organise, but reaped rewards eventually. They had to cover their own costs, of course. Molly also did well, but not through seminars. She, like Ted, had built up a regular, loyal clientele over the years.

They had to pay for everything themselves. After all, they were running their own businesses. It suited the company that their consultants were self-employed. It meant they had to pay for all their own stationery, literature, telephone usage, computers, even their desk space. It also meant the company could get rid of them whenever they liked. Peremptory dismissal was common. There was no jurisdiction in regard to self-employed people, no protection for them. The company did not have to pay employer's liability or establish pension funds for their consultants, who had no claim to sick pay or holiday pay either. The company's view was that they were privileged to be working under the company licence. On one occasion, a group of consultants had gathered together and tried to establish a trade union for the self employed, but they got little response from the consultants, who were all terrified of that peremptory dismissal should they be even suspected of not toeing the line.

Insurance companies in those days, and many still in these days, worked on the old principle of "divide and conquer". Everyone worked for themselves. Each month the Top Performer was recognised. One of the branch manager's jobs was to encourage the others to outdo the top performer by whatever means. "Dog eat dog"!

Bill's seminars were inspirational. All his preaching skills came to the fore, and he delivered wonderful sermons about savings and investments. He held his audiences in thrall. Nobody knew that, technically, he was unsound. The important thing, from his perspective, was that he managed to make money out of it, to survive. Aziz was, of all of them, technically the most brilliant. And he was a good teacher. He spent many hours patiently coaching Padraig, Garth and Eleanor, who were relatively new to the industry.

Ted, Molly and Bill knew it all already, or so they thought. The only one of the three who was really suspect was Bill, but he got away with it.

There were sexual undercurrents in the office, of course. With six men and four women, it was inevitable. Molly flirted outrageously with Andy, Padraig flirted with Eleanor. Garth was mesmerized by Eleanor. He had never met a woman like her before. Her very voice fascinated him. Ted rather liked Ann. Aziz kept himself to himself, but watched everything and missed nothing. And Bill did not appear to have much sexual drive. Perhaps that had something to do with his weight. He must have been at least eighteen stone. All the men, of course, appreciated Jane who was young and very pretty with a beautiful body.

It quickly became apparent that Gavin, this new, incredibly able Branch Manager, all of twenty-eight years old, had become fixated on Jane. He virtually drooled in her presence. She, flattered at being the object of the Manager's attention, agreed to go out with him and, in no time at all, they had become an item. She radiated happiness, and he radiated testosterone. He could not manage without sex for more than a few hours at a time. So he and Jane were like rabbits, bonking at every opportunity. They would go out together in his car at lunchtime rather than join the others in the pub. Frequently they were caught in the office in the evening by a consultant returning from a client appointment. They spent their weekends together. Jane still lived at home with her parents. So she and Gavin were always first in to the office in the morning, where they were able to spend an hour alone together before anyone else arrived. Needless to say, they were caught several times by the cleaners. These days Jane started each day with her cheeks all red and shiny.

Most of the flirting that went on in the office was light hearted. Molly was a little too earnest in her pursuit of Andy. But Andy was not interested in Molly anyway, so it did not matter. Garth's interest in Eleanor blossomed. She, herself, a good looking woman in her forties, was not unsusceptible to a little flattery and attention. In fact, she craved affection. She had been alone – not counting the children, of course – for too long. Garth was married, which constituted a problem. "What the hell" she thought. "He's a big boy. He knows what he's doing". She went out with him – just to the pub, and then for an Indian meal afterwards. He kissed her goodnight, on the lips, but not too long. It was good. "Harmless" she told herself. But, as things do, the relationship progressed. Pre-menopausal, Eleanor's sex drive was very strong, as it is with so many women in that stage of life. It is as if their bodies are telling them "This is your last chance". Her very proper exterior hid a passionate inferno internally. Garth had never known anyone like her. He was besotted.

Padraig loved Eleanor dearly, as did Aziz, both in a brotherly sort of way. Aziz asked her out one evening. He cooked her a Persian dinner, which she loved, and then took her to task. "Eleanor, what are you doing?" He asked. "Garth is so entirely unsuitable for you".

"Oh, Aziz" she said. "It's the excitement, the thrill, the passion. I know it's wrong, but I can't stop". "Passion?" he asked, puzzled. "Haven't you ever known passion, Aziz?" "No. Never". "What? You've really never known passion?" She turned towards him, astonished. "But, Aziz, I thought you were married once. You must have known passion then." "No. It was a girl I met at University. It was a marriage of convenience, I suppose. We got on. But it only lasted five years". "Poor Aziz" she said, stroking his cheek. Eleanor was very fond of Aziz. He was honest, conscientious, and genuine, but imagine never having known passion.

Padraig also took it upon himself to have a word with

her. "Be careful" he said. "You're getting in rather deep, and Garth is married." He also spoke to Garth. "Look here, man, you're not doing yourself any good, or Eleanor. It's got to stop". Garth was miserable. He really loved his wife and family, but was out of control. He thought of Eleanor all day long, was only satisfied when he was beside her in the office or with her out of it. He had a conscience. The stress of trying to hold down a job which, at the best of times is hard, the constant deception of his wife, his passion for Eleanor, took their toll. He became more and more withdrawn, got spots. "Spots!" thought Eleanor. "He's a grown man".

There was a County Show on at the weekend. Gavin suggested that he and Jane, Garth and Eleanor all went together. They did. It was fun. There was so much to see and do. But, all of a sudden, there was Garth's wife, Susan, with the children. Garth, embarrassed, tried to make light of it. Eleanor drew right back. She did not want any trouble. Gavin made a lot of noise about it being a company outing, and Jane, who liked Eleanor, looked daggers at Garth's wife.

The following Monday, Eleanor received a telephone call in the office "You fucking cunt!" Eleanor recoiled. "You've been at it with my husband. I've got his gun. I'm coming after you. I'll fucking kill you." Well-bred Eleanor said "I'm so sorry you feel like that". The woman was incandescent. "You fucking cunt" she repeated "you should see me when I'm dressed up, when I've got my make-up on. He can't take his eyes off me". "Well, that's the difference" said Eleanor "I don't have to make an effort to make an impression." And she put the 'phone down. Slightly worried by the conversation, Eleanor decided not to tell Garth about it. She did not really think his wife would come after her with a gun. Nonetheless, she was careful in regard to her comings and goings, ensuring there was nobody about, locking her car and house doors at all times – which was so out of character for her. She wondered what to do about Garth. Despite knowing that it was wholly irrational, she was by now besotted with him. Her "little bit of rough" her children called him. She could no more end the relationship than fly to the moon. Matters, however, were taken out of her hands. Garth, increasingly stressed and ill, handed in his notice. He left the company immediately, never to be heard of again. Gavin was hurt; he had formed a relationship with Garth. From similar backgrounds, he felt they had something in common. Garth's wife was definitely the controlling force, and it would have been her decision that he would not have anything to do with anyone from the company again.

Gavin's own relationship with Jane was not going particularly well. She had started to make demands such as one would expect in a serious relationship; he should meet her mother; they should spend all their weekends together. Jane was innocent, naïve. Gavin had no intention of settling down. He wanted to play. He was seeing a lot of Eliza again. He did not see any reason to tell Jane. Anyway, he was interested in another girl he had met, Amy. "Hot totty, that" he thought. "I'll have her".

Jane, not understanding his point of view, continued to pester him. Why could they not spend more time together? Why could she not join him when he went out with his mates? Why did he keep her hidden away from his friends? He hit her. He punched her in the face, and left. She, in tears, got a taxi home. She hid her black eye from her mother, but the consultants in the office noticed it.

They were simply relieved that Gavin's love life was taking up so much of his time. They were shocked, of course, at his treatment of Jane, and made sympathetic noises. However, self-interest was the predominant force. It meant that he left them to their own devices to get on as they pleased, without interference. Jane had taken to coming in to work late, frequently tearful, frequently with bruises. Gavin treated her abominably. He also started treating Ann very badly. He was rude, discourteous; he shouted at both of them, threw paperwork at them, berated them for non-existent minor misdemeanours.

Molly was becoming agitated. She was not getting the support from Gavin which she needed. She visited his office on a number of occasions, and always left dissatisfied. His knowledge of Trust law, of compliance, was negligible. How could this office run with such an asshole in charge? It was the general consensus of the consultants that they would get no support, no assistance from this man. He was, for them, a liability rather than an asset. They were all having problems with him. He was a lazy, deceitful light-weight. It incensed Aziz that he lied boldly and openly to the Directors in regard to progress at the Branch. He regularly claimed business for himself which had been brought in by the other consultants.

Andy visited the office for the regular monthly meeting. Everyone was enthusiastic about Gavin as branch manager. All was going swimmingly; they could not have a nicer fellow in charge. They were not going to give either Andy or Gavin the opportunity to withdraw their licences. They both held the power. Aziz said it was self-preservation. Gavin's chest puffed up. He really believed that they believed what they were saying. Andy's chest puffed up too. Gavin had been his choice. The managing director had wanted someone else, but Andy had won that one. Reality was that Gavin was now showing his true colours. He was "a nasty piece of work", as Eleanor said.

Molly, whose knowledge of Trust law was extensive, was having a run in with Gavin. They were ensconced in his office, and had been there for quite some time. He was shouting at her. She was shouting back. Those outside could not quite make out what was being said, but the tone of their voices was unmistakeable. She emerged fuming. She had brought in a substantial piece of business written in trust for inheritance tax purposes. Gavin, having no knowledge of Trust law, would not sign the business off. "He's a fucking asshole" said Molly. "He shouldna be here at all" and, collecting her things, she went home. Once at home, advised by her husband, Molly telephoned Andy and lodged a complaint against Gavin. She refused to return to the office whilst he was there. She was not prepared to be insulted by him any more. The things he had said to her were disgraceful. She, a senior consultant of considerable standing, expected the company's full support. She was hauled up in front of the Board of Directors to be disciplined, at Andy's insistence. Molly had been friendly with the Directors for the past fifteen years.

The next day, Gavin was in a filthy mood. He decided to take Bill to task for not having brought in enough business that month. Bill stood up for himself, answered back and, before anyone knew it, there was a brawl with Gavin throwing punches at poor old Bill, who was far too large to sidestep, but who retaliated valiantly. They were pulled apart by Aziz and Padraig. Bill was shaken to the core. Aziz got him a coffee and poured a little brandy in it from his secret "emergency" flask. Gavin retired to his office. The others were in an open plan area. Gavin shouted to Jane from his office "And you, you useless waste of space, get me a hot chocolate". The powdered chocolate was in a big tin by the kettle.

Jane sat quietly counting to ten. Then she got up, took the tin of chocolate powder into Gavin's office, and tipped the contents all over him. She picked up the glass of water on his desk and tipped that over the chocolate powder – all down his double-breasted, pinstriped wide-boy spiv suit. He was on his feet, roaring. She turned and ran out of his office. Grabbing her handbag, she left. "Look at me; look at my suit. It's ruined" screamed Gavin. Those consultants left in the office, unaccustomed to all this physicality, pretended not to notice him. They were concerned about Bill, who they knew had a bit of a heart problem. Nobody said anything, but they closed ranks. Unanimously, without a word, they decided that, by sticking together, they would overcome any managerial interference. None of them trusted Andy to be any better than Gavin, but Aziz took it upon himself to "have a word with Andy". Aziz was nothing if not diplomatic.

Andy called a meeting. He sat beside Gavin, and told everyone that Gavin had his full support, that Molly would not be returning. She had been a trouble maker. Neither would Jane be returning. Gavin had cancelled her "pass" so that she could not re-enter the premises. She had been useless as an administrator, and they were well off without her. As for the run-in with Bill, he said, it had been a misunderstanding, and Gavin deeply regretted it. Gavin smirked. Aziz, Padraig, Bill, Ted, Eleanor and Ann fumed silently. Andy and Gavin said their "goodbyes" and left for the afternoon.

The consultants had no respect for either Gavin or Andy. They were both buffoons, but they had to put up with them. Andy and Gavin had the power to throw them out of their jobs at the drop of a hat. That was a lot of power in the hands of very inadequate people. They had no management skills, no training. It was never considered by the Board that such training was necessary; besides, it was very expensive. Andy had been a salesman, quite a good one, prior to becoming Regional Manager. Nepotism reigned throughout the industry. Favourites got the jobs. Frequently it went to their heads, and they became puffed up with their own self-importance. Very particular skills were needed to manage a team of self-employed consultants. By the very nature of the work they do, they have to be self-sufficient, innovative, adventurous. They lived on their wits and on their nerves. They were not accustomed to being commanded or led. Their lives were generally a roller-coaster of elation, and depression, depending on when they were earning and when they were not. They had to be cajoled, encouraged. More than anything they needed product training (which they got in some degree), encouragement, support when the going was tough. They did not need a constant barrage of criticism, of having their noses rubbed in the success of others when they were failing – which is what tended to happen.

It is extraordinary how much can change in just a week. Eleanor said "For God's sake, let's get a drink. We need it". Ann volunteered to stay behind and man the telephones.

They were horrified, on arriving at the pub, to find that Andy and Gavin were already there ahead of them. "What are you having?" Andy asked. He insisted on buying a round of drinks. Slapping Bill on the shoulder "Come on, Bill" he said "no hard feelings". Bill choked. Eleanor, when she had a quiet moment, asked Andy if she could have a private meeting with him. "I'm far too busy right now" he said. "Later, maybe". "Andy, I've got a client to see in an hour's time. I can't do it later" she said, and walked away. She was angry. All this nonsense going on in the office, and Andy was ignoring it.

Eleanor nudged Padraig. She had spotted Jane coming in to the pub. Andy spotted her, too. Desperately trying to maintain the status quo, he called "Jane, what are you having?" It's on me". "Thank-you Andy" she said "I'll have a pint of Guinness". Gavin looked uncomfortable, but could say nothing in Andy's presence. Jane walked over to them, taking her Guinness. Andy was standing, Gavin was sitting in a chair. Standing behind Gavin Jane coolly tipped her glass of Guinness all over him. The sticky liquid ran right down to his shoes. In front of Andy he could say nothing. The second suit ruined in a week, by the same silly tart. He'd kick the living daylights out of her when he caught up with her. His face was red. He seethed. He went to the 'Gents' to try and clean up. Andy, trying to be jovial, laughed. Jane smiled "Thank you, Andy" she said "I've been waiting to do that. 'Bye everyone" and off she went. Eleanor ran after her. "Be careful, Jane. If he finds you, he'll really have a go". Jane laughed. "He won't find me".

Gavin got a taxi home. The others breathed a sigh of relief. Andy joined them. Eleanor had to go. As she was leaving, Andy said "Eleanor, I'll see you in ten minutes". The whole week had been a complete mess. The atmosphere in the office was awful, and they had that crap excuse for a manager; Andy was as bad. "Fuck off, Andy" she said "I've got a meeting to go to. I've told you already". And she left, conscious that she could not afford to be late for this particular client. It was Thursday. Only one more day to go.

On Friday morning both Gavin and Andy were in the office, an unusual occurrence. Andy called Eleanor in. They were both sitting behind Gavin's desk. The office was small, just one other chair. "Sit down" said Andy, as if he was talking to a child.. Eleanor had no idea what they wanted. Andy started talking; in fact, he did virtually all the talking. He accused Eleanor of having been drunk when she went to see her client the previous evening – she "stank of alcohol"; at the Christmas party she had undressed the chairman; she had insulted one of the directors. The list went on and on. Eleanor was shocked, incredulous. She, herself, could not get a word in edgeways. Was this man sane? All the others out in the main office could hear what was going on. Padraig popped his head round the door. "Say, guys" he said "I think Eleanor could do with a little moral support here. I'd like to come in and sit with her". "Get out" yelled Andy "or you'll lose your licence too". Padraig withdrew. He had a wife and family to support.

As he spoke, Andy became more and more agitated.

"Nobody" he screamed "Nobody has ever told me to fuck off before. That is absolutely the worst thing you could say to anybody. Only tarts use that language". Eleanor was a little ashamed of what she had said, but she had said it without malice. It is not what you say, but the way that you say it which matters. She was crying. She was being subjected to so much vitriol. She got up, and started to walk out. She was simply not prepared to take this abuse. The man was mad. "Sit down. You will NOT walk out of here without my permission" shouted Andy. By now she was utterly shaken, utterly cowed. She sat down. The verbal abuse continued for another fifteen minutes. Occasionally Gavin chipped in but, on the whole, he remained silent, smirking. "Oh God, the ignominy of it. Why can't I stop crying?" thought Eleanor. She does not know how, but eventually she got out of that office. Padraig gave her a big hug; Aziz patted her on the shoulder; Bill and Ted bustled about making her a cup of tea, pulling up a comfy chair.

"The trouble is," said Aziz "that when they behave like that, we have no redress". "Perhaps we should have joined that trade union" sniffed Eleanor. "Gavin's always getting at Ann, too" said Padraig. "She's been in tears on several occasions. He calls her all the names under the sun, tells her she's fucking useless, shouldn't be in the job". "They're both misogynists', not worth worrying about. Forget about them. Go home, and have a nice weekend, and it'll all blow over by Monday". Eleanor went home. Aziz and Padraig had a quiet word with Andy, but it made no difference.

Once home, Eleanor telephoned Molly. Molly was not surprised at what had happened. "That's what they did to me. You'd better watch your back. Remember, I've been with the company for fifteen years. I thought the directors were my friends. When it comes to protecting their own, they close ranks. I thought they'd stand by me, but they didn't. If they don't support their management, they lose face. So the consultants get it in the neck all the time." "Surely we can do something, if we join ranks" said Eleanor. "Don't count me in" said Molly. "I've had enough. I can't fight any more." Molly was still in a state of shock; she was on tranquilizers, crying all the time. Her husband, fuming, was helpless.

On Monday morning, Eleanor reluctantly went in to the office late. Ann was there, very quiet. Gavin had already been in and given her her notice. She had to be out by lunchtime. "Why?" asked Eleanor. "He says I'm useless" said Ann. "I don't believe this" said Eleanor. She commiserated with Ann. "You'll get another administrative job easily. Good administrators are hard to come by. And you'll get into a much happier office" She said.

On Eleanor's desk there was a letter addressed to her. It was from Andy. He considered her position in this office now to be untenable, and she was to be transferred to Swindon. But that's a hundred miles away, she thought.

Now there were only Aziz, Padraig, Bill and Ted left in the office. Jane and Molly had gone; Ann was leaving, and Eleanor was also effectively leaving. It would be impossible for her to commute a hundred miles every day, and she knew it.

The four of them agreed that Aziz would be their spokesman, and they called a meeting with the Chairman of the company. Without embellishment, and in simple terms, Aziz explained what had happened. It was extraordinary that, of the original eight people in the office, there were now only four left. All those who had gone had been sacked, and they were all women who had been doing a good job. The revenue lost to the company by the sacking of Molly and Eleanor alone was in the order of nearly three quarters of a million pounds a year.

Three months later, neither Gavin nor Andy was with the company. Aziz, Padraig, and Bill remained. Ted had taken early retirement. It was all too much for him. Jane had decided to go into nursing. Ann had found another administrator's job with a company where she was treated really well. Molly was still in the throes of a nervous breakdown, which it took her many months to recover from. Eleanor, unaware that she also was having a nervous breakdown, found herself crying daily, unable to cope. She had not found another job, and was desperately trying to sell her house before it was repossessed by the building society with whom she had a mortgage. It had taken two misogynistic bullies just a few days to totally change the course of four women's lives.

Aunt Maisie's Crystal

Jack climbed the hill slowly. He was rather inclined to breathlessness these days. He carried a shopping bag in each hand. It was a pity the bus stop was at the bottom of the hill. He lived further up, in a council bungalow which he had shared for twenty-five years with Maisie, his beloved Maisie.

He still missed her terribly, but had worked out a routine to cope. He went to the graveyard on Sunday morning, Tuesday morning and Friday morning. It was two bus journeys away, and took the greater part of the morning to get there and back. He had long talks with Maisie, discussed everything with her, told her all the news. He always took a bunch of fresh flowers, and he trimmed the grass around the grave with a little pair of scissors. He had planted a dwarf rose bush in the middle of the grave, and a circle of crocuses and pansies around it. He kept the grave immaculate. The white headstone would sparkle in sunlight, and the flowers were always bright and vibrant. Maisie would like that.

At Christmas and on birthdays, he would send a card to his son, Bill. "I hope you are keeping well, Lad, as I am" he would write. There was never a mention of the loneliness, of the heartache, of the fact that Bill never bothered to come and see him, or even to contact him at all.

Jack had been a gardener. Always a modest man, he worked hard, was never indebted to anybody, was courteous and polite. He doffed his cap as he passed others in the street. When he met someone new, he would look them in the eye and shake them firmly by the hand. Tall and lean, slightly stooped these days, he had big, bony, gnarled hands. He helped neighbouring widows with their chores, looked after their gardens for them. He kept himself busy but, all the same, he still missed Maisie, It was not the same as when she was with him.

He had married Maisie when they were both eighteen. It was before the war. There was not much time then, to waste. So they got on with it, and got married. He had never regretted a single day. Maisie was beautiful. The war years were a living hell. He had had a bad time of it, lost many friends, been involved in horrific hand-to-hand fighting. Maisie joined the land army. A farmer's daughter, she took to it naturally. She was a strong girl, and worked hard. She wrote him glowing letters about home, the harvests, life in the village. It was all normal and familiar. It kept him sane in an insane world.

Half way up the hill Jack stopped, putting his bags down. He was wheezing, trying to draw breath. He felt peculiar. Something was wrong. His chest was tight, it was hurting.

His eyes rolled as he fell.

Jack could hear sounds around him, but he did not want to open his eyes. It was peaceful cocooned in sightlessness. Some one was saying "He's lucky; he's got a strong constitution. He should pull through, although the next few hours will be critical." Where was he? What was happening? He was warm, cosy. His last memory was getting off the bus with his shopping on the way back from the cemetery. His brain felt fuzzy. It was not quite right. He opened his eyes, someone was leaning over him "Jack, Jack" she called "Can you hear me? You're in hospital, Jack". With an effort, he turned towards her. Who was she? What was going on? "You're in hospital, Jack" she repeated "You've had a little stroke. We're keeping you in here for a few days". He opened his mouth to speak, but he could not. He tried again. What was happening? Why couldn't he speak? Jack was confused, so tired. He fell asleep.

He dreamed. He dreamed of Maisie, of their wedding day. They had married in the village. They had walked to the church. Maisie was a picture. She had on a long white dress with meadow flowers in her hair, and she was carrying a posy to match. Her mother had made the cake and sandwiches, and they had a reception in the village hall. All the villagers had helped to deck it out with flowers and swathes from the hedgerow. Tom, the accordionist, had played all evening, and they danced and sang along. It was the happiest day of his life. Jack smiled in his sleep. They had opened their presents in front of the guests. It was all part of the fun, part of the joy. They had been given so many things to help them start their new life together. A shiny new kettle for the range, some thick woollen blankets, a tea set, a sewing machine. But Maisie's delight was the big crystal fruit bowl her mother gave her. He could see her now, her round dark eyes shining, as she said "this bowl will never be without fruit, for the rest of our lives". It was symbolic.

For their honeymoon, they went to Bognor where they stayed in a Bed and Breakfast. Neither of them had been to the seaside before. They had a grand time frolicking in the sea. They returned to the village. Jack was a gardener up at the big house; Maisie looked after the children. They were lucky. They were both employed. Jack had rented a terraced two bedroomed cottage for them. He dug the garden and planted flowers for Maisie, and vegetables. They always had their own fresh vegetables. He planted an apple tree and a pear tree, gooseberry bushes, red currants and black currants, strawberries. Maisie wanted a greengage tree, so he planted one of those. They would not go short. Maisie, with her new sewing machine, made curtains for the windows, cushions for the chairs, and a lovely warm bedspread for the bed. They were ideally happy.

In the big world outside the village there were rumblings, rumours, discontent, fear even. People rushed home after work to listen to the news on their wirelesses. Jack and Maisie did not have a wireless, but the housekeeper at the big house told them every day what the wireless had said. That awful man, Hitler, was causing trouble in Germany. No doubt we will be going to war soon. Then it was announced. "We are going to war" the housekeeper said. "Men all over the country are rushing to sign up". She could remember the first world war. "I thought all that had ended. God help us. Life will never be the same again".

Jack and Maisie discussed it. They were unanimous in their decision that Jack must do what he could to help his country. He signed up. He told the master at the big house, who patted him on the back. "Well done, lad" he said gruffly. "You're doing the right thing". For the time being, Maisie would stay on at the big house. She had three children to look after. They were lively, robust. They spent the mornings with their tutor whilst Maisie cleaned and tidied the nursery, did the mending, and any other chores. In the afternoons she would take them for a walk. She loved showing them the country, the wild flowers, the trees, and berries. They would collect pussy willow, old man's beard, bulrushes, apple blossom, wild roses, depending on the time of the year, and display them in vases in the nursery. Sometimes they would collect watercress from the bottom of the stream for their sandwiches at teatime. She had formed a particular bond with the eldest girl, Geraldine.

Geraldine had made Maisie tell her all about the wedding, the presents she got, the cottage. Geraldine was so curious. Maisie laughed as she told Jack, who would be going off to war that very day. Neither of them understood the full implication of what he was doing. They both thought, as did the rest of the country, that it would all be over in a matter of months, and they would get back to normality again.

The following Christmas, Maisie received a present from Geraldine who always called her "Aunt Maisie". "It suits you" she said, "much more than just Maisie. I shall always call you Aunt Maisie". Remembering Maisie's love of her crystal fruit bowl, Geraldine had given her a crystal swan. Maisie was thrilled. The years went by, and every year Geraldine gave Maisie another crystal piece: after the swan came a dolphin, an eagle, a woodpecker, a cockerel. Jack made Maisie a special cabinet in which to keep them. The shelves were mirrored, and there was a light in the back, so that all the crystal reflected the light, and in prisms sent waves of bright and beautiful colour around the room.

The war went on and on. Maisie worried constantly about Jack. Every woman in the country worried about her man. They all dreaded receiving "The Telegram". "Lost in action". "Died in action". It made no difference what it said, it was still the same. Life changed at the big house. It was turned into a sanatorium for those poor devils suffering from shell shock to recuperate. The family withdrew to a cottage in the village, and Maisie joined the land army.

It seemed like a lifetime later that Jack came home. He brought with him two pairs of beautiful silk stockings for Maisie, who had worn only ankle socks throughout the war. Maisie was so relieved to get him back in one piece. The children at the big house had all grown up now, and no longer needed Maisie. The old housekeeper had retired. So Maisie was offered the housekeeper's job. She accepted it with alacrity. Jack got his old job back, except that he was now "head gardener". Their joint salaries had increased, and life was getting back to normal at last. There was still rationing, but it was being phased out gradually.

Maisie, nine months later, bore Jack a son, Bill. Jack was so proud. When he went down to the pub in the evening to have his regular Guinness, he beamed as everyone congratulated him, and nobody let him buy a single drink. He went home a little the worse for wear that night. Maisie, in bed with the baby, did not mind. She understood Jack, and felt he needed some release from time to time. The next day, the doctor came. He told Maisie and Jack that there were complications during the birth, and that Maisie would not be able to bear any more children. They were philosophical; they had their beautiful Bill, they had their home, and they both had work. It would be greedy to ask for more.

The years went by. Bill grew and grew. He was a bright lad, good at schoolwork, but not particularly interested in the land. He was more inclined to have his nose in a book. "A regular bookworm, our Bill" said Maisie. But Bill and his father were becoming estranged. Bill was ambitious. At school, he was learning about all the wonderful opportunities which existed out there in the world. He could not understand his father's contentment, lack of curiosity. Apart from the war, and the occasional seaside holiday, his parents had never left the village. They had never had holidays abroad, had never gone to London even. Bill, a restless teenager now, found them dull, boring. He spent less and less time at home. Maisie and Jack carried on their lives as before. They did not know anything else. Eventually, Bill left home and went to University. Jack and Maisie were so proud of him. Quietly Jack would tell his mates "Our Bill. He's doing well".

Bill did not always come home during the holidays. He went off on work experience ventures. He taught children in Ghana one year, he helped build a village hospital in Tanganyika another year. He trekked through Nepal. He did lots of things. He sent his parents postcards from time to time. They were so immensely proud of him, but they did not believe in bragging. Jack was saddened by his son's attitude. He did not understand it. He had always imagined they would be close, do things together. But he never let anybody know of his sadness, particularly not Maisie.

Bill got his degree, a first. Jack thought he would burst with pride. He put on his only suit, and spruced himself up, whilst Maisie wore her wedding hat when they went to see him getting his Degree. Bill pushed them over in to a corner, away from his mates. "We don't want to spend our precious time together with them" he said. And he took them to a pub round the corner where they had lunch, well away from the other students and their families.

"I've been offered a job in computers" said Bill "in London. "Oh, Dear, that sounds lovely" said Maisie. Jack nodded. "Well done, lad" he said "I suppose that means you'll be moving out for good". Jack accepted everything that was thrown at him. He never complained, but he would miss his son. They already inhabited different worlds.

Jack and Maisie returned to their cottage and breathed a sigh of relief. They did not much like venturing out into the bigger world. Maisie was very tired. She had not been too well lately, and got tired often. Jack made her a brew. Private people, unaccustomed to displays of emotion, they did not discuss Bill. They did not need to. Very proud of him, they understood each other.

As the years passed, Maisie got more and more tired. She had to give up her job. She found the stairs difficult.

She was losing weight. Eventually Jack suggested it might be a good idea if she were to see a doctor. He diagnosed cancer. (The big "C" as it was whispered around the village). It was the doctor who got social services to organise a flat for them so that Maisie would not have to cope with stairs any longer. Leaving their little cottage was a wrench, but it was a relief as well. It had all become too much for Maisie to manage. Jack did his best to help her, but he was working all the time. Maisie died in her sleep. She was fifty-one.

Jack retained a quiet dignity throughout the following days. He called Bill, arranged the funeral. He appeared composed, self-contained. The neighbours were kindly, made him cups of tea, brought him cakes and sundry other goodies. They congratulated him on managing so well. But Jack was distraught. Each night, in the privacy of his bedroom, he sobbed and sobbed. Bill had gone back to London after a couple of days. He was sad to lose his mother so early, but he had already cut the apron strings and was now leading his own life. Jack had shaken his hand when he left "Thanks for coming, Lad" he said "I shall miss your mother. Keep in touch, won't you."

Jack, in his hospital bed, appeared to be distressed. He was crying out, thrashing about. The nurse shook him by the shoulder. "Jack, Jack" she called "Wake up. It's alright. I'm here". Jack awoke. He looked around him in a daze. "You've in hospital, Jack. Do you remember?" asked the nurse. He was frantic. He tried to speak, but only garbled rubbish came out. He was frightened. What was happening? How long had he been here? He could not ask. He could not speak. Jack grabbed the nurse's hand, pointing, but she did not understand him. He wanted a notepad so that he could write. Utterly frustrated, he sank back into the bed, mentally climbing inside himself. He could no longer communicate with the world around him.

After Maisie died, Jack had kept the flat spotlessly clean and tidy. Maisie would have wanted him to. He took especial care of her crystal collection, still in the special cabinet he had built her. There was the crystal fruit bowl. Since she had died, he no longer had the heart to put fruit in it. There were all the crystal animals she so loved. He dusted them carefully every day. He never broke anything. And the cabinet, lined up opposite the window, collected all the sun's rays as they entered the flat. He would sit in the evenings, just watching those shining crystal pieces. They were really beautiful, and Maisie had loved them.

The hospital doctor told Jack that he could not go home to the flat. A place had been arranged for him in a home. It was local, not too far away, and his friends could come and visit him. Jack did not want to go into a home. He wanted to go back to where he belonged, where Maisie was still waiting for him. Ever since she died, he had felt her presence in the flat, particularly when the sun was shining on the crystal. It never went away. Jack tried so hard to speak, but it was still only garbled rubbish. Tears rolled silently down his old weatherbeaten cheeks.

The doctor had somehow found out where Bill lived, and notified him. He came to see his father. Jack was so small now, so frail. His helplessness was heartbreaking. He tried valiantly to speak to Bill. Finally Bill realized what he wanted. He produced a notepad and pen. Jack just about managed to write "CRYSTAL" in large, wavering capital letters. It was a huge effort for him. Fortunately Bill understood what he wanted.

Jack was transferred to the home on Christmas Eve. They all thought he would be happier there than in hospital during the Christmas period. He was given a room of his own, and Bill had brought in the whole cabinet, with all the crystal. It was opposite the window, just as it had been at home, where the light would catch the glass as it shone through. The staff in the home were kind. They had put up Christmas decorations in Jack's room, and Maisie's wedding photograph. For the first time in weeks, Jack smiled as he sank back into the pillows. He ate a good meal, and slept.

When he awoke, it was early morning. It had been snowing outside. He had not let the nurse draw his curtains the previous evening. He never slept with the curtains drawn, preferring to meet nature head on, so to speak, as soon as he woke. A weak winter sun was shining through the window, the crystal lights were dancing all around the room. He wanted to get out of bed, to go to the window, but, since the stroke, Jack had not been able to walk properly. One of his legs simply would not do as it was told. He heard a blackbird singing and, looking towards the window, there was Maisie outside, looking in. She was smiling at him, saying something. He sat up in bed, stretched out his arms towards her. "My Darling, wait for me. I'm here. I'm coming" he called. "Come on then, you big Loon" she said, stretching her own arms out towards him. "I've been waiting for you for so long. I see you've kept my crystal nice. I'm glad of that". She was laughing, teasing him. He got out of bed. Approaching her, arms outstretched, he took her in his arms.

The staff had made an effort for everyone in the home. The breakfast trays were adorned with sprays of holly and glittering red and silver baubles, and the staff all wore red pinnys to cheer things up. Each breakfast tray had a little wrapped present on it. Jack's was a nice bar of soap. The carer opened Jack's door. She blinked. The multi-coloured lights from the crystal were dancing all round the room in a brilliant display. And then she saw Jack. He was slumped in the chair by the window, crystal light dancing all over his face.

He was smiling. It was Christmas Day.

They telephoned Bill and said they were sorry to inform him his father had passed away peacefully in his sleep. Bill was more upset than he cared to admit. At last he was maturing; he was beginning to understand that Jack's contentment with his lot had nothing to do with materialism, but more to do with being at peace with nature, at peace with himself. At the funeral, Bill made a vow that he would never, ever let his father down. Perhaps he understood at last his father's nobility, strength, and courage.

CREEPING JESUS

Sandra and Tim were just about surviving financially. He had a Representative's job now, not making much money, but just about enough. He had been big in the city until he was made redundant, and then he was never again able to get similar work. Everyone told him he was too old. Sandra also worked as a sales representative, three days a week, and as a doctor's receptionist two mornings and three evenings a week. They enhanced their income a little by letting two of their bedrooms for Bed and Breakfast from time to time.

The house was very old, sixteenth century, and had received no tender loving care for at least a hundred years. Most of the woodwork was rotten; they had dry rot, wet rot, woodworm everywhere. The roof was a disaster. Every time it rained, they ran around in the loft, which was also living space, placing buckets, saucepans, any bowl available under all the leaks. Tim pulled out from some of the holes pieces of old newspapers and magazines, all pre-dating the forties. They had obviously been stuffed up there by previous owners in the hope of staying the flow of water into the house. The master bedroom was in the loft. When the previous owner sold the property to them, she had laughingly told them how, when in bed, the wind howled around the bed, and it felt so cosy all tucked up in a warm duvet. They should have taken her literally.

They decided that they would have to sell the place. It was huge and, now that the family had left home, far too big for just them. But they knew that nobody would get a mortgage on such a dilapidated property, so Tim, useful about the house, decided to restore it in his spare time. He started with the roof. As with all old properties, as soon as he discovered and started to tackle one problem, another revealed itself. The end result was that the whole roof came off, tiles, timbers, beams, joists, even the floor had to be lifted and replaced. He worked on the roof at every opportunity he had. Sandra helped him. They would both be up there, above the scaffolding, replacing tiles when friends and neighbours would pass by below. One local wag offered to put out chairs and charge the passing public to sit and watch them. The roof took four years to complete.

In the meantime, Tim also completely rebuilt the bathroom; inner walls, ceiling, lighting, plumbing, floor, bath, hand basin, loo, all had to be replaced. He replaced the sitting room floor. It had been beautiful old elm, boards eighteen inches wide, which would have been put in when the house was originally built. It was nearly all eaten away by woodworm. To replace the damaged elm would have cost them six thousand pounds. Elm is now so scarce. In the sixteenth century, of course, when the house had been built, it had been prevalent. Tim found a reclamation yard which agreed to exchange what good elm he had left with sufficient old pine planks to replace all the elm. So they at least managed to replace the sitting room floor for virtually nothing.

Tim replaced all the plumbing in the house, he put in central heating. An electrician came in to do the wiring. The downstairs entrance hall, the kitchen and larder, and the dining room still had to be renovated. All the restoration work was costing a fortune, which they did not have. So they mortgaged, then they remortgaged, and then they remortgaged again. The house was a financial drain. And now it was a real struggle to maintain the mortgage payments each month. They were both permanently exhausted and, somehow, they needed to make more money. They could not afford any small luxuries such as going out to dinner, the theatre. They could not afford holidays. Neither of them could remember when they had last had a holiday. What a silly idea! Sandra even felt guilty about buying herself new underwear when she needed it.

A friend, Sharon, telephoned Sandra "Are you still doing Bed and Breakfast?" "Not really, the house is in too much of a pickle" said Sandra. "I've got a friend who needs a room for just a couple of nights. Can you help him out? He's a real gentleman, very rich". "Well, why does he not stay at an hotel?" asked Sandra, who did not want the hassle of preparing a room, and all it entailed on top of everything else that was going on in the house. Doing Bed and Breakfast was not easy. It meant everything in the house had to be kept scrupulously clean and tidy. With builders coming and going, that was virtually impossible. "He doesn't like hotels. They're too impersonal". Sandra needed the money so, reluctantly she agreed. She would expect to be paid weekly, in advance. The money would help pay for all the building materials they had to buy.

The man arrived. He was huge, well over six feet tall, and broad. He appeared to be nervous. "Built like a brick shit house" thought Sandra, warily. She showed him to his room. He was happy enough with that. She offered him tea and biscuits, which he accepted. His name was Jo Smith, he told her, and he would get the money for the rent in the next couple of days. He was out of breath after climbing the stairs. Clearly, the man was not fit. She estimated he was about sixty years old, but he might have been younger. Too polite to remonstrate over the rent, Sandra retreated.

Sandra was a good cook. Each morning Jo enjoyed a large full English breakfast. Early on, he pointed out that he was Jewish. Sandra was concerned. She was giving him sausages and bacon for breakfast. "I'm not a practicing Jew" he said, "The bacon's fine". Whilst he ate, Sandra would chat to him, as she would to any Bed and Breakfast guests who were alone. Initially, he was reluctant to be drawn into conversation, but gradually he thawed. Organising guests' breakfasts prior to rushing off to work was always a struggle for Sandra, but somehow she managed. Jo showed no desire to move on. Sandra, always courteous, was reluctant to bring up the topic of rent, which had still not appeared. Occasionally, Jo would say "I must get you the rent money, I owe you two hundred and ten pounds", or whatever it happened to be at the time.

He was very bitter about women, referring to them all as "Doris", a term Sandra had never heard before, but she presumed that, as he came from the East End, it was colloquial slang. He told her he had been married twice before. He saw his children from the first marriage. He had first been married to the sister of a famous television star. She left him because he devoted all his time to work, and not to her. In the divorce settlement, she got the family home which he had worked so hard to get her. Apparently it was beautiful, and worth, even then, a million pounds. He did not see the children from his second marriage. That wife had really taken him to the cleaners. She was German and they had lived in Germany.

He said he had started off life in the East End. At the age of twelve he started to sell umbrellas in Oxford Street. He would leave a box full of umbrellas and a flask full of hot soup with the newspaper vendor, who was also Jewish, walk up and down the street with three umbrellas on each arm, and not go home until he had sold the lot. He always wore an old pair of shoes, full of holes, he would plead hunger. Being, in those days, undersized and skinny, the ladies in particular were kind to him, not only buying the umbrellas, but giving him tips as well. He gave everything he earned to his mother, who put it into savings for him. He had a hard childhood. His parents were not happily married. His father was a womaniser, his mother resorted to drink. His father bought his mother expensive gifts to compensate for his womanising, but she became more and more bitter. They fought. His father was a car dealer, and made a lot of money, but he was tight with it. He invested everything – usually in property, and had quickly become a multi-millionnaire.

By time he was seventeen, using his earnings, saved for him by his mother, Jo was able to buy his first house. Still living at home, he rented out the house and saved the income. He started to dabble in cars like his father. As soon as he was able, he joined the local boxing club. He certainly looked like a boxer. His hands were the biggest Sandra had ever seen.

By the age of twenty-one, Jo had a small property portfolio. He had started buying up anything he could get cheap, in large quantities, and selling it on. He was making money! Jo's father would not help him. Jo felt that his father, who had had a long and bitter struggle to achieve success himself, was jealous of Jo's rapid ascent. Jo's Uncle helped him financially, so that Jo was able to establish a considerable business buying up container loads of imported goods and selling them on. Jo's relationship with his uncle was better than that with his own father. For many years he had bought and sold just about anything, especially property. Jo produced a photograph of his father, a small wizened man in open-necked, collarless shirt and braces. He did not look a pleasant character. It appeared that, throughout his life, Jo had had a love-hate relationship with his parents. He spoke bitterly of them, but still clearly craved their approval, their affection, right up until they died.

Jo would spend hours every day, just sitting in his room. Sandra felt sorry for him, and started giving him lunch, dinner in the evening, when she was at home. He was partial to Brandy, drinking a whole bottle on his own in one evening. Sandra asked him how it was that he, a successful businessman, spent so much time alone in his room. He had a computer game up there which he played endlessly, something to do with racing cars. He told her that he was waiting for important international 'phone calls. He had organised his businesses in such a way that he had very little to do himself. He trusted implicitly the men he had put in charge. He did have two mobiles, Sandra had to admit. He would say "Didn't you hear my 'phones ringing in the night? I was worried in case they would wake you up." Needless to say, neither Sandra nor Tim had ever heard Jo's 'phones ringing, daytime, evening or night time. Jo never had any money on him, or precious little. The rent was still not forthcoming, and the extra meals and Brandy were costing Sandra a lot of money, which she could scarcely afford. One Sunday, he asked them if they would join him for lunch at a local pub. To his credit, he bought them a delicious lunch, and would not let them pay for the drinks. Perhaps his money has come through, thought Sandra.

Sharon had started coming round, to visit Jo in his room. The two of them spent hours ensconced together. They were talking business, Jo said. Sharon brought him a litre of milk every time she came. She told Sandra that he liked milk, and it was good for him. She brought him take-away meals, cake, sweets, sugar, honey. Sandra noticed that Sharon, who had always dressed in such a way as to cover up everything, never revealing any flesh at all, was now dressing in a much racier manner; string strap tops, feather boas, high heels and short skirts. It was all very odd. She teased Jo about Sharon. "I think she's taken a shine to you, Jo" she said. "Na, she's not my type" said Jo.

Jo told Sandra and Tim more and more of his past. After his first wife divorced him, Jo had bought a villa in Gibraltar, and a night club, which was very profitable. He ran his businesses (he had four) from Gibraltar. All sorts of well-known people came to his night club, sportsmen, footballers, boxers, film stars, entrepreneurs. He was well known in Gibraltar, had his own chauffeur and housekeeper. He entertained regularly on a grand scale. Whilst in Gibraltar, at the night club, a woman had approached him and chatted pleasantly enough. She, unbeknown to Jo, had decided that she would marry him. She started to stalk him. She got her way, and they were married.

They moved to Germany, but Jo still kept the night club and his villa in Gibraltar. They bought an hotel in Germany, which they decorated in the best possible taste; lots of red plush and a pure white grand piano, crystal chandeliers, the whole works! Jo's attention span was limited and, tiring of the hotel, he sold it. Needless to say, he made a fortune.

They moved to England. Jo continued to make money. He set his wife up in business selling German gateaux to large hotels. It was a successful business, and all went well for a while. All went well, that is, until she found another man. She had to get rid of Jo. That is when she reported him to the police both in Germany and the U.K. for fraud, and when he got locked up in prison in Germany. Whilst he was in prison, she had forged his signature on documents, sold all the German and U.K. assets, and made off with the lot. She also reported him to the tax office in the U.K. for tax evasion. He had been tried in the U.K. and got off. But the judge told him that, should he ever set foot in the U.K. again, he would be locked up. She had taken two and a half million pounds off him,

According to Jo, she and her boyfriend are now living comfortably on his assets. He did manage to keep the night club and villa in Gibraltar.

Jo liked to go out to the local pub for a drink in the evening. There, he would sit on the high stool at the bar telling stories. King of the Castle! He was a good story teller, and kept everyone in hoots of laughter. The centre of attention, he was in his element. He appeared to take particular pride in his Jewishness. He once said he had changed his name by Deed Poll to Jo le Zimmerman Smith. His favourite story started "When I was in Burma, fighting in the war, at the Battle of Pork Chop Hill ...". Bridie, the landlady intervened "But you're not old enough to have fought in the war, Jo." Jo roared with laughter. Of course he was not old enough. And Port Chop Hill did not exist either. He appeared to be generous, although he managed to buy very few drinks for other people. Most people, because he was telling such good stories, would buy him drinks. He quickly became known in the pub, and offered one group of young men a holiday at his villa in Gibraltar. Delighted, they accepted, and excitedly booked their flights.

The pub, he told Tim and Sandra was up for sale, and he, Jo, was going to buy it. He had had a long chat with the owners, Bridie and Keith, and an agreement had been reached. "Why do you want a pub, Jo?" asked Tim. "I don't want it for myself. I'll put a manager in. It'll be the first acquisition of my new property portfolio." Tim and Sandra knew Bridie and Keith, who were thrilled that Jo was going to buy the pub. They were retiring, had found their perfect little dream cottage, and could not wait to start their new life. They were so excited.

Brian, a lorry driver with a bad back, drank regularly in the pub. He hated his job. His back caused him a lot of trouble. Jo said "I need a chauffeur. You can drive for me." Brian was delighted. "When can you start?" asked Jo. "Oh, I'll have to give a month's notice" said Brian. "Right. Do it." Said Jo. Brian gave in his notice, and was looking forward to his new job, driving a nice comfy Mercedes for Jo.

Jo moved incredibly quietly for such a large man. Tim, spotting him in the street one day, tiptoed up behind him. Jo turned around immediately. He had been aware of Tim's presence. "I've learned to keep my eyes skinned" he said "I always look out all around me, and especially behind". Tim was impressed. Sandra once had been given a terrific fright by Jo coming up the stairs into his room whilst she was making his bed. She had not noticed him. He made her jump out of her skin. "I've always moved quietly" he said. "My mother used to call me Creeping Jesus."

He told them how, in Gibraltar, he had been approached by some Russian businessmen. They wanted him to change money for them. They wanted him to go to Russia and discuss the deal. He went. But he was afraid. Dealing with the Russians is dangerous. These were the Mafia. And he did not want any more trouble with the police. He drove back from Russia across Europe. He was carrying large amounts of money in a briefcase (millions of roubles). The car broke down. He was terrified. Somehow he got the car on its way again, and made it back to Gibraltar, where he went straight to the police and handed over the money

– all but one bearer bond! Consequently, the Russians put out a contract on him. He still had the Bearer Bond, but did not dare cash it. Sandra and Tim were bemused. Was this man real? Tim, who had considerable experience of underground movements, said that, if the Russians really had a contract on him, he would be dead.

Jo said that he had bought a small house in the north of England, and had kept a low profile there for the past three years. He had got involved with another woman. He spoiled her, lavished gifts on her, and he was relatively happy. But she started to take him for granted. He told Tim about all the wonderful cars he kept up there, in the north: a Jaguar, a Bentley, a Mercedes. He had an old Audi for when he wanted to keep a low profile.He had become incensed when, having bought the "Doris" a car of her own, she was dissatisfied with it and started driving his car instead. Then, when he had been out, she told him, there had been four strange men walking about in the field adjacent to the house. They seemed to be very interested in the house. They were dressed in business suits.

Not waiting to say goodbye, leaving everything behind – passport, wallet, cards, everything, Jo jumped in the Audi and fled. He was, as he assured Tim and Sandra, protected by the police. He only had to make a telephone call, wherever he was, and they would come to his rescue. This is how he had arrived, penniless, at Sharon's. But he was waiting for funds to come through. As soon as a container was sold, he would have money, not just a few pounds, but thousands. He made a hundred thousand pounds' profit out of each container. Actually, he was now worth eleven million pounds. He had worked it out in bed that night.

Sandra and Tim needed another ten thousand pounds to finish off their roof. Here was this man boasting about his wealth, and he could not even pay them the rent he owed. He seemed to have no idea of the incongruousness of his chatter.

He had several containers, he said, (at one count it was thirty-two) sitting in the docks. He was furious that they were being held up. "All this anti-terror stuff" he said. "They are taking so long to pass containers through. There's a huge backlog at the docks". The containers were full of furniture, white goods, computers, televisions, telephones. He had a warehouse up north where everything would be stored, prior to disposal. He had to pay the warehouse men, the storage, the drivers, the lorries. He was in a desperate situation. If he could not sell even one of the container loads, he could not raise the money to pay his staff. If he was worth so much, said Sandra, surely he could raise funds from somewhere. She was incredulous. He must have money if he was a multi-millionnaire. He had a banker in Gibraltar, he said, Otto, who was also a special friend and his financial adviser. This friend looked after all Jo's money for him. Because of the court case, Jo did not dare to be seen to have any money in England, in case he got caught by the tax office again. So Otto handled everything.

Sharon was experiencing financial difficulty, so Jo was going to set her up in business. Sharon found a little shop. She told Sandra how grateful she was, and how excited she was. Jo was such a wonderful man. Jo would have all Sharon's stock in and ready for her to catch the Christmas market, and Sharon would never look back.

Jo would disappear mysteriously at night – going to business meetings, he said. Who has business meetings at night? When questioned by Sandra, he said he was meeting the C.I.D. in regard to the men who had been in the field outside his home in the north of England. They had been Russian Mafia members, who had followed him. Should the C.I.D. find out that he had told her anything at all, all hell would be let loose. She was not to say a word to anyone. His connection with the police, with the C.I.D., was highly confidential.

Jo was not a well man. He was always breathless, could scarcely walk fifty yards, and on a couple of occasions, had asked Tim to take him to hospital because he felt so unwell. He said he had lung cancer, but he still smoked like a chimney. He also had heart problems. He said his specialist had told him that an operation was the only solution, but that he, terrified of the knife, had refused to have the operation, and so the specialist told him that his days were numbered. Reality is that he was at death's door. "Why on earth don't you have the operation, if it will make that much difference?" asked Sandra. "Oh, I've got nothing left to live for" said Jo, "I'm not interested in life any more. I don't care if I live or die." A bit melodramatic, thought Sandra. He did not take any drugs, any pills. He said he wanted to speak to Tim, to have a meeting with him and Sandra.

Sharon was still visiting Jo every day in his room. She would slip up the stairs so quietly that Sandra never knew whether she was there or not. She always brought a two litre bottle of milk. That's an awful lot of milk for one man to drink every day, thought Sandra.

Jo, Tim and Sandra sat around the dining room

table. Jo said "As you know, I've got businesses based in Gibraltar. I'm not well, and I want to ease up a bit. I've told you I'm starting to buy up more property over here. I've already got six houses and several business premises. They've all been let, so I've got an income stream there. Since I've been here I've got to know you rather well, Tim, and I like what I see. You're good at management. You'd be no good at what I do; I'm a wheeler-dealer, but I need someone to manage my businesses for me. I think you're the man for the job. You know about property, about renovation. I want you to manage my property portfolio" said Jo. "Will you do it?" Tim, who hated his present job, and was capable of so much more, was interested. "Tell me more" he said. "I'll tell you what I'll do" said Jo "I'll advance you twenty thousand pounds. That'll give you enough to get this house finished. If you work for me, I don't want you being distracted by building work. Why do it yourself, when you can pay someone else to do it? You'll have to come with me to Gibraltar" said Jo, "and Sandra had better come too. We'll leave on Wednesday next, I'll organise the tickets. I'll get Otto to book everything."

Tim then realized his passport was out of date. "Don't worry" said Jo "I know where you can get a new one within hours. We'll have to drive to Newport in Wales. There's a passport office there where you can get a new passport immediately, but it'll cost you something. So the next morning Tim and Jo drove off to Newport. The round trip, together with the cost of the passport cost Tim nearly two hundred pounds, money he could scarcely afford. He gave a week's notice at work, and, by Wednesday the following week, was out of work.

The following Monday Jo went off to London – to borrow some money from his uncle, he said, just to keep things ticking over until they got to Gibraltar. He stayed away on Tuesday, was not answering his 'phone. Wednesday came and went. Tim and Sandra were packed and ready to go to Gibraltar. Jo eventually reappeared on Thursday. He said he had been in hospital for the past forty-eight hours; he was too ill to travel anywhere. It would have to wait. "I want you to find me a warehouse down here, in the south, Tim" he said. "It's got to be big enough to take twenty container loads of stock at a time and it has to have secure parking for container lorries". "Sandra," he said "I want you to find me an outlet to sell the stock, probably through computers. I shall need at least five telephone lines, and eight computer connections. Can you arrange it?" Tim and Sandra went to work and, within a fortnight, had found premises which Jo approved. He put in offers to buy each of them.

The following weeks were difficult for Tim and Sandra. They were by now very suspicious of Jo, who still had no money. There were always excuses when Sandra asked him for the rent: he was waiting for the money to come through from one of the containers, which he had just sold, but the man who had bought the stock had disappeared. Jo had his strong arm men out looking for him. They would get the money, have no fear. He told horrific stories of what he had done to people who had thwarted him in the past. There was the chip shop owner whose head had been thrust into his own chip fryer; there was the butcher who had ended up hanging on one of his own meat hooks. So it went on. Then he was waiting for funds to be transferred from Gibraltar. This time he said

Otto had stopped the transfer because of the tax office.

Tim and Sandra were struggling financially. Tim now had no job. Jo offered to buy their house off them. They could go on living there, but he, Jo, would own it. That idea did not appeal to Tim and Sandra. They thanked him politely but declined the offer. They still wanted to believe in Jo, because his offer of work to Tim was so attractive, but they found it more and more difficult. They were very worried.

Then someone came round to see Jo. Jo told Sandra it was a man from whom he, Jo, would be renting a very nice flat just down the road. The man had come to hand over the keys. Sandra thought "well, he must have money, then. Nobody would let him rent a flat without having first put down a deposit. I'll damn well make sure I get the rent out of him before he goes" That afternoon Jo went out.

The following morning, Sandra went to make his bed. The bed had not been slept in. The room still smelled horrible. It had smelled horrible ever since Jo had arrived. Sandra thought it might be the tobacco he was using; she could not place this particular smell. It was strange because Jo gave every impression of being clean, fastidious even, about cleanliness. She opened the window as wide as she could. As usual, the room was neat and tidy, just a packet of biscuits and a jar of honey left out. "What's he done with his play station?" Sandra thought. She had a strange feeling. She opened the wardrobe – empty! She opened drawers. She found old mouldy cake, a plate full of mouldy take-away, another half eaten cake, sweet wrappers, an old dish of what looked like cauliflower cheese. How disgusting! And that was it. There were no clothes, no personal items, nothing. He had gone.

A cupboard was built into the wall of the bedroom. It was a very old cupboard, and, internally, went round behind the door. Sandra opened the cupboard. Initially, she saw nothing, but then, behind the door something caught her eye. She looked. What on earth was he doing, stacking up all those milk containers in the cupboard? What was in them? She could not believe what she thought she was seeing. She opened one of the bottles. She grimaced in disgust. She was right. Jo had left thirty-one two litre milk bottles full of urine in her cupboard. What was he thinking of? She could understand that he might get caught short in the night, but why not empty the bottles in the morning? How disgusting! She called Tim. They emptied the bottles. The smell permeated the whole house. It was revolting, nauseating. They both retched. They put the bottles into a bin liner, and Tim took them down to the local tip immediately. Even the carpet smelled of Jo's urine. They pulled it up and burned it. Sandra scrubbed the room thoroughly, using strong bleach wherever she could; they kept the windows wide open for weeks and weeks before that terrible smell gradually disappeared. Curtains, bed linen, cushion covers, chair covers, all were washed over and over again. Gradually the smell dissipated, but it took a long time.

Jo was never seen in the village again. It was two weeks before Christmas. Sharon's business venture came to nothing; the lads who had booked their tickets did not get the holiday of their dreams which Jo had promised them; Bridie and Keith did not sell their pub; Brian, having given up his lorry driving job, was out of work; the man whose flat Jo was about to rent, was left with an empty flat; the estate agents from whom Jo had been buying the warehouse and the shop had been let down; Tim, having given up his representative's job, was out of work. Sandra, having looked after and nurtured Jo for several months, was out of pocket. Nobody had got an actual address for Jo, nobody knew where he had come from, or where he had gone. Where had he moved on to? Who was he preying on now?

Bridie and Keith are still running their pub; Brian has gone back to his lorry driving job; the boys lost the cost of their flights, but feel they got off lightly by comparison with others; Sharon still lives in hope of having her own business one day; the estate agents managed to sell the relevant properties anyway; Tim found another much better job six months later. Jo owes Sandra a lot of money, and she will never forgive him for the damage he did to so many people.

His legacy of sixty-two litres of urine, Sandra thought, was entirely appropriate. He had fooled them all.

Jazz at South Bridge

Sandy had been a paratrooper; he then applied to join and was accepted by the S.A.S. They trained him and trained him. The training had been uncomfortable, harsh. On many occasions he had thought himself about to go mad or to die. But it was necessary. All his own personality had been drained out of him, and replaced with hard, blind loyalty to Queen and country. He would have died happily for his Queen. He was tough. He was hard, and, for as long as he was careful and watched his back, he was invincible. Light and wiry of build, strong and fit, with the natural short temper of the redhead, he was, even prior to joining the army, a dangerous adversary. The most important thing he had learned in the army, he felt, was to control his temper. But they had taught him so much more than that. He would never fully understand what they had done to him.

Soon after joining the army, Sandy married his

girlfriend. They had been dating since he was eighteen and she seventeen. He adored her, and, with her, was soft, sentimental, a ball of marshmallow. He would do anything for her. She was convinced he was the most wonderful man in the world. She was glad he went into the army; she was really proud of him, and he looked so handsome in his uniform. They posed happily for their wedding photos, smiling; they had the whole world ahead of them, the whole of life, and it was all going to be rosy.

Sandy and May moved into married quarters at the barracks, and soon started their little family. First John came along, then Maisie. May, herself, got on with the other wives at the barracks. She quickly joined the mothers and toddlers group, the baby-sitting circle, and did all the things so necessary to a young mother who knows she will be left alone for many months of the year. She integrated. Sandy would disappear for weeks, sometimes months at a time. Frequently he could not even tell his family where he was going. When he returned, he never spoke of where he had been, what had happened, other than that he operated in a very small team and that he trusted his mates with his life. He had one mate in particular, Steve. He owed his life to Steve, and Steve owed his life to Sandy, so they were quits. May was grateful to Steve.

Sandy had fought hard, fast and dirty. He had killed, maimed and, where necessary, tortured. It was his job. Inevitably, unable to discuss these matters at home, and hardened by his training and experiences, he had become very insular, self-contained. He was jumpy, morose; he cried out in his sleep. May was finding it more and more difficult to relate to him, to find some common ground.

She no longer felt that they were communicating, that she could understand him. He even distanced himself from the children. He, himself, when pushed, acknowledged that he was now a different man. To himself, but not to May, he also acknowledged that he no longer felt anything for either May or the children. His feelings were dead. He was uncomfortable when he came home, restless. He wanted to be out on operations again. His job had become an addiction.

Inevitably, the marriage disintegrated and, after two more years without any improvement, Sandy and May agreed to part company. He wanted access to the children. By now May was actually afraid of her own husband. He was cold, calculating, distant. She was frightened of what he might do to the children (not that he had ever hurt a hair of their heads). She retained custody. He had access, but only in her presence. He was very bitter about that.

After the divorce, Sandy was sent off on yet another operation. He knew that this one would be particularly dangerous. Steve went with him. Sandy was glad of that. It proved to be the worst campaign Sandy had ever been on. This was guerrilla warfare at its worst. You could never tell where or when the bastards might pop up. They trusted nobody. They had to watch out for land mines, bombs, mortar attacks, day and night. The terrain was harsh. Boiling heat in the day, freezing temperatures at night, they were constantly thirsty, hungry, watching their backs as they worked their way slowly forward. They did not sleep for days on end.

The worst thing possible happened; the patrol was caught in an ambush one night. It was chaos, dark as pitch. They had to fight bitterly for their lives. The noise was incredible, guns, shouting, screaming men. In the darkness they could see nothing but flashes of tracer and fire. Eventually they got away. It was the closest shave they had yet encountered. Exhausted, they went to ground and fell into their dug out hollows in the sand. It was some minutes before Sandy realized that Steve was missing. There was nothing they could do now. He dozed fitfully, too tired to sleep. The patrol retraced their steps the next morning, particularly careful and alert. They found Steve's body. Badly beaten, battered, bruised, bones broken, his throat had been slit. An old rope was still tied tightly around what little was left of his neck. Clearly he had been dragged along by the rope. His hands were tied behind his back. He had been missing just fifteen hours. Sandy showed no emotion. The shutting down process he had already started was now finalised. He would never again experience life as pleasure, pain, emotion. He had become a fighting machine, no more, no less.

When Sandy returned, it was the end of his two year tour with the S.A.S. He returned to his regiment as a Corporal.

Harder, tougher than the other soldiers, cold, remorseless, most of them were slightly scared of Sandy. He did not fit in, keeping himself to himself, speaking little, and only when absolutely necessary. He never laughed, he never smiled. In the Corporal's Mess he ate alone. Behind his back he was referred to as a "that miserable bastard", but none of the other soldiers dared challenge him. They always behaved towards him with the utmost respect. None of them could know that Sandy's only remaining purpose in life was to avenge Steve's death. This he had sworn to do when he found the body, and he pursued the idea relentlessly. Out on exercise, Sandy deliberately broke his own ankle. He smashed it over and over again with his own bayonet. Thereafter he walked with a limp, and was invalided out of the army.

He was a civilian now, with no ties, and a small army invalidity pension. Provided he was frugal, and he was, it was just about enough to live on. He had not seen or contacted his family since the divorce. They were merely distant memories, not a part of his life any more. Alone, quietly, without fuss, he travelled back to where Steve had died. He made his inquiries. He knew how to get information out of people. The man who had killed Steve, he established, was called Asad, but Asad had left the country. Where had he gone? No-one was sure. Maybe Egypt; maybe Indonesia, maybe Iran, maybe Afghanistan or Pakistan. The trail had apparently run cold.

Sandy spent the next six years travelling around the world, looking for Asad. Had he not been fanatical in his desire for revenge he would readily have agreed that he was being ridiculous. How was he to find an individual called merely Asad, amongst all the people in the world. He was still fit, wiry. Capable of living on a sparse diet, and self-sufficient, he wanted for nothing. He despised those who needed luxuries. He travelled light. He had covered Afghanistan, Pakistan and Iran. Now in Egypt, he could still find no trace of Asad. He worked his way from Egypt to Singapore on a container ship. They were carrying coffee. From Singapore he would make his way to Indonesia.

Singapore harbour is one of the busiest in the world. Hundreds of container ships come in daily from all over the world, bearing everything from white goods to precious spices. These vessels are frequently anchored in banks six containers wide and several miles long. Bum boats (tiny little pilot boats) shuttle to and fro amongst the container ships, fetching and delivering crew who wish to go ashore.

A Bum boat came out to pick up the crew and take them into town. They were taken straight away to Geylang, the red light district. The girls were like candy, so many to choose from, all beautiful, fragile, delicate. There were boy-girls too, just as beautiful as the real girls. It was virtually impossible to tell which was which. They beckoned, enticed, clamoured for Sandy's attention. They sidled up to him, crooning, stroking. He brushed them aside. He had long since given up girls. They held no charm for him. As for the boy-girls, they disgusted him. He would willingly have killed them all with his bare hands, given the opportunity. Saying his goodbyes to the crew members, who naturally wanted to stay in Geylang, he held his temper and moved quickly through the district.

The air was balmy, humid, tropical. After the dry air of Egypt, Sandy liked it. Travelling for five years, in predominantly arid terrain, had taken its toll. His wiry frame was thinner. His skin was ebony brown, dehydrated, etched with deep lines. His red hair was greying rapidly. With his dark eyes, he could pass for a local. He found a food court where he could get a good meal for three Singapore dollars. Then, his hunger sated, he started to walk the streets. He was indifferent to the sheer opulence of the shopping malls, with their designer chic, their marbled floors and waterfalls. He was more at home amongst the Chinese shops and market stalls of

Chinatown. But still he did not notice their charm, the little shrines set out for the Hungry Ghosts, the jugglers, the lanterns shining brightly, the people. He was, after all, a machine. The Singaporeans were friendly, kindly people, on the whole very polite. He found a bar, dark and cool inside, where he could sit with a Tiger beer, observing the world outside. There were so many people in Singapore. He could be anonymous here. He wandered on again. Time meant nothing to Sandy.

He found himself on Boat Quay, a centre for tourists and, especially, Europeans. There were pubs, restaurants, clubs there. Chinese red lanterns were strung along the quayside, reflected on the water. The restaurants and bars all had tables outside, lamps, lanterns. Light was dancing everywhere. It was very pretty, but that was lost on Sandy. The first pub he came to was The Penny Black. It was open to the quayside, with tables and chairs set outside as well as inside, as is so often the case in Singapore. There was air-conditioning inside. The wooden floor, plain tables and chairs set well apart from each other, and small red lampshades on the chandeliers, the long bar, and gently whirling fans added to the air of lost colonial security. There were Europeans here, plenty of them. It had been some time since Sandy had been in the company of his own kind. He had forgotten how large Europeans can be. He sat outside The Penny Black, people watching. For the first time since he could remember, he found himself vaguely interested. Maybe it was the air which was making him soft. It did not occur to Sandy that the task he had set himself had been so impossible that both his mind and body were weary, worn out.

His search for Asad had so far proven fruitless. There

were many men called Asad. But none of those he found had killed Steve. He had approached his search with an intense ferocity, obliterating all feeling other than hatred for the man who had killed his best mate. Now, sitting outside The Penny Black, in a quiet moment of reflection, he admitted, deep down inside himself, that his intensity had diminished, that he really was becoming weary of the search. It was not often that Sandy had such moments of honesty with himself. He rarely allowed himself to think at all, other than in regard to his crusade for revenge, and his own survival. Six years of travelling rough had taken its toll. He rose, wandered on, past Harry's Bar, to the end of the quay where he found a rickshaw driver, who took him to a cheap hotel in the Indian Quarter. His room was windowless, but clean and air-conditioned. He had a shower. That was all he needed. He would investigate a passage to Indonesia tomorrow. He slept well that night.

He arose early, as was his wont, and went out. The Indian quarter was fascinating. He wandered along the narrow streets, already happily garlanded with colourful wares. He stopped for a fruit juice – the fruit thrown into a blender, then poured into a glass. It was cold, refreshing, delicious. He noticed the taste of the fruit. What was happening to him? He spent the whole day wandering, observing, watching. Singapore appeared to be a happy place, and safe. This was something Sandy was unaccustomed to. He had been watching his back for the past twelve years. He found it difficult to relax, to adjust. Before he was aware of it, night had come. Perhaps he would stay in Singapore for a few more days before going on to Indonesia.

In the evening he returned to The Penny Black in Boat

Quay. He liked it there. He moved next door to Harry's Bar. He liked that too. Nobody bothered him. He spoke only when necessary and only to the little waitresses. They were pretty, sweet, attentive. At midnight, he rose to return to his hotel. Walking down Boat Quay, he spotted a "Jazz at South Bridge" sign. Curious, he climbed the stairs. On the first landing there was a restaurant entrance. Some primeval instinct drew him on. He could not explain it, but Jazz at South Bridge beckoned strongly. He climbed another flight, and found the Jazz Club.

As soon as he opened the door he felt at home. The air was cool. He could hear the liquid strains of a saxophone. There was an ante room, then a bar, then a lounge where the public could sit, drink and listen, looking into the inner sanctum where all the action was taking place. This inner sanctum was well equipped, walls and ceiling clad in sound boards, bare wooden floor. There was a black lacquered grand piano, a Vibraphone, a Pearl drum set, a range of various guitars propped casually against the walls, recording equipment, speakers. Small, comfortable blue chairs and tables were arranged hospitably in a semi circle, and flickering tea lights were everywhere. The main lighting was soft, even, high level. In his lost life many, many years ago Sandy had quite liked jazz. He bought a whisky on the rocks, and went in to the lounge. Four musicians were playing, the saxophonist, a pianist, a bass player and a drummer. They were good! Really good! The sounds were liquid gold. He felt the tension draining out of him. Not much, just a little! He stayed for an hour, sipping his whisky quietly, and slipped away.

Walking along, minding his own business, Sandy felt a light tap on his forehead. Historically, he would have lashed out and knocked out any individual who touched him. This time, he did not. Standing in front of him was a large Sikh gentleman, who said "Forgive me for interrupting your thoughts, Sir, but you are an unhappy man. Your face tells me. Your destiny is written in your face. For the past many years, you have lost your soul. Yes, you have lost your soul; but you are about to find it again. You will become a changed man. Your mission is over." He wanted money, of course. Sandy felt in his pocket and produced two dollars. The Sikh bowed and walked away. More disturbed by this encounter than he cared to admit, Sandy nonetheless felt happy about it. The words "Your mission is over" played on his mind.

Before he knew it, Sandy had been in Singapore for a whole fortnight. He had established a pattern whereby he wandered the streets by day, frequently sleeping in the afternoons, and going on to the bars in the evening. It astonished him that there was no fighting in the bars. There was heavy drinking, but no fighting, no theft. Night after night Sandy found himself drawn back to the Jazz Club. He could not explain why. If asked, he would have said that he simply felt comfortable there.

The musicians were laid back, casual. They took turns to play, inviting each other. Between sessions, they would wander amongst the audience, talking, introducing themselves. There were many very young players, all nationalities, Singaporean, Japanese, Chinese, English, American, German. Race, colour, creed, none of these things mattered. For Sandy, it was refreshing. On Sunday nights particularly, the Club filled up with youngsters eager to show their prowess. All were encouraged, invited to play, to sing, whatever they wanted to do. The standard was high, excellent.

Still monosyllabic, uncommunicative, Sandy, nonetheless, found himself gradually drawn into occasional conversation. He asked the bass guitarist why he had a five string guitar, why he sometimes used a fretless guitar. He was actually interested. There were different kinds of saxophone, a tenor sax., an alto sax. He had not previously known that. The Club owner, Eddie Chan, played the vibraphone – very well.

Enveloped in liquid sound, wrapped around like a blanket, Sandy was changing. He began to notice the people around him, occasionally to speak to someone. Whereas, previously, everybody had given him a wide berth, instinctively acknowledging that here was a hard and dangerous man, people were now approaching him, talking to him. The music, so gently, was beginning to finger his soul. Eddie Chan approached him. "You like jazz?" he asked. Eddie owned the club. He was a small, compact man with a round face and smiling eyes. He was always courteous, always friendly. He had such an air about him that Sandy instinctively took to him. Eddie lived for his jazz. It was the love of his life. He told Sandy his story.

"I was born in Hong Kong, but grew up here, in Chinatown. Well, in those days it was equivalent to Harlem in New York now. I always loved music, especially Rock and Roll in the late fifties. Someone gave me a jazz record for my birthday, Dizzie Gillespie. That was it. I was twenty-two years old in Chinatown in the last days of the British Empire. Actually, that was funny. When the British left, we had a grand national parade here in Singapore. But we had no band. All the bands had been

British. We could not have a parade without a band, so the government rounded up all the night club musicians and somehow turned them into a band sufficient to play in the parade. We had our own band!" Eddie laughed delightedly. Sandy actually smiled. "We have so much talented youth here in Singapore" Eddie continued "the schools started their own bands. The standard was high. But these youngsters, playing at school, had nowhere to go and play when they left. So much raw young talent was lost, wasted." Eddie laughed again. "Actually, I worked hard and qualified as an architect. I'm a good architect. I built my own house. But jazz is my first love."

He became serious, pensive. "Jazz – coincides with my own philosophy of life. Jazz is a discipline, a serious music form; but it leaves room for individuality, for improvisation. It encompasses all music. Of course, styles are changing. Jazz was born of the old negro slaves. It was an outpouring of grief. It is an urban discipline. It is a discipline of the inner cities, not the suburbs. We have an Academy of Music here now. We've only had it for a couple of years, but music students have to learn about jazz. They now have written jazz music to work from. In the old days it was passed on by ear." He smiled wryly. "What really bothered me was those young people with such talent and nowhere to play. So I started the Thomson Jazz Club – a club for youngsters who wanted to play jazz. Ah, that was a good move. The Club is a non-profit club, and has grown and grown. It is now the Thomson Institute." Eddie was very pleased with what he had achieved in Thomson Street.

"This Club makes no profit. It is a struggle to survive. We need publicity, but I shall never give it up. It is my life". Eddie stopped for a while, and drank. "What I want" he said "is for Singapore to be a beacon for the rest of the world, a jazz beacon, a centre of excellence. We'll do it, you'll see. I have worked hard all my life. It took so much energy to get everything up and running, but I have not stopped yet." and he ended the conversation. Eddie was a genuine philanthropist. Sandy had never previously met anyone like that.

As Sandy was leaving that evening, Eddie called him over "You will come back here again and again" he said. "You won't be able to help yourself. And gradually, the music will heal you, you'll see". Sandy was disturbed; first the Sikh, then Eddie, talking about finding his soul, about healing. What utter rubbish!

The following evening, Sandy left Singapore for Indonesia. He went to Bin Tan Island. His Visa had run out, so that he could no longer stay in Singapore. After a week in Indonesia, making desultory and half-hearted inquiries about Asad, Sandy met a holy man. He told Sandy his quest was over. Sandy could not understand all these fortune tellers (as he saw it) telling him to give up. What business of theirs was it, anyway? He was angry, but not physical. Nonetheless, he returned to Singapore.

He returned to "Jazz at South Bridge". Eddie Chan spotted him and raised a glass in a smiling toast of welcome. Sandy was approached by a girl. He had seen her there before. "I've seen you here before" she said. "I presume you like jazz". It was a formal, polite conversation opener. "Yes" Sandy said evasively. She took no notice of that, and continued to chatter happily at him. He did not want to be drawn into this. He was uncomfortable with such proximity. But, somehow, he stayed, and was drawn into the conversation.

That night, before he slept, Sandy thought that he might just stay in Singapore. What he did not yet realize was that he was beginning to feel, to appreciate what he saw, tasted smelled. It had been such a long time. He was beginning to find his soul again.

Lightning Source UK Ltd.
Milton Keynes UK
UKOW02f2155311016
286566UK00001BA/3/P